A Bit of Razzle Dazzle

HOLIDAZE IN SALEM

A Bit of Razzle Dazzle

HOLIDAZE IN SALEM

KELLY ELLIOTT

A Bit of Razzle Dazzle
Book 4 Holidaze in Salem © 2023 by Kelly Elliott
Cover Design by: Graphics by Stacy
Interior Design & Formatting by: Elaine York, Allusion Publishing
(http://www.allusionpublishing.com)

For more information on Kelly and her books, please visit her website www.kellyelliottauthor.com.

To all my little witches out there, *A Bit of Razzle Dazzle* is the last book in a four-novella series! If you haven't read the first three, I suggest you go back and read them. Since this is the continuation and conclusion of Hollie and Lucas's story, you'll have a better reading experience if you're familiar with the first three books.

Now, let's get this story going, shall we?

Prologue

Hollie

Lucas is in denial.
I know he possesses magical powers.
So, I decided to do what I do best.
Create a spell to do all the rest.
A little razzle dazzle potion is needed, stat!
Unfortunately, it also affects the new guy in town: Matt.
Oh dear...my sister now has to babysit a man
who doesn't know witches and warlocks are part of the plan.

Chapter One

Hollie

I paced back and forth, my mind whirling as I wondered what I was going to do. The front door opened and Lucas walked in. When he saw me, he came to a stop.

"What's wrong?"

"Sarah's in trouble."

Lucas frowned. "What do you mean she's in trouble?"

Sighing, I dropped onto the sofa. "I can feel it; something's wrong. I think she needs me."

Lucas sunk down into the chair. "I keep getting these odd feelings that we need to be back in Salem too," he said. "I don't know how to explain them."

My brows shut up. Another clue! I pulled out my phone and jotted it down.

Lucas frowned. "I had the strangest dream last night that when I held the baby, I could understand his thoughts. It freaked me the hell out. I think it was because you read my mind yesterday and answered my question before I even asked it."

"Interesting," I mused, taking another note in my phone.

"What are you doing?"

"Making notes."

"About?"

"Baby stuff."

Lucas let it go, but I knew a part of him sensed that I wasn't making notes about the baby.

"Well, I guess this is good timing then," he said.

"What is?" I asked as I placed my hand on my belly. I was twenty weeks pregnant and finally really starting to show.

The baby moved, and I gasped. "She's moving!"

Lucas put his hand where mine had just been. When the baby kicked again, he looked up and laughed.

"Strong kick. Has to be a boy."

With a shake of my head, I said, "Nope. I'm telling you, it's a girl."

"I'm telling you, it's a boy."

Rolling my eyes, I changed the subject and asked, "What's good timing?"

"I've been asked to go back to Salem by the mayor. Apparently, they were excavating for a new parking garage and they found an archaeological site that looks like it dates back to when Salem was colonized."

"Oh wow! What about the dig site here?"

Lucas smiled. "We've discovered a lot, and it's been fun, but I'm ready to head back home. I miss our families, and I want to be back in the states since you're getting further along in your pregnancy."

I hadn't told Lucas I was homesick, but there were so many times I'd longed to see my mother, aunt, and sister. Plus, I missed Kristin and Shawn. I knew Lucas missed everyone as well.

"When are we heading back?" I asked.

"How soon can you be packed?"

We hadn't bought much while we'd been in Ireland. The flat we rented was fully furnished, so there really wasn't anything we'd needed to get.

"I can be packed in an hour!"

Lucas laughed. "I'll look up tickets and book us a return flight."

Hugging him, I felt my emotions start to bubble up. I knew it was hormones from the pregnancy. When I drew back, he wiped my tears away.

"You've missed home?" he asked.

I nodded. "I have."

He placed his hand on the side of my face and ran his thumb over my cheek. "Thank you, Hollie, for standing by my side while I did this."

I covered his hand with mine. "I'd stand by your side no matter what."

He leaned in and kissed me. When he broke the kiss, he rested his forehead on mine. "I love you, Hollie Payton."

Rubbing my nose against his, I replied, "I love you too."

"Call Sarah and tell her we're on our way."

My phone rang, and we both laughed.

Lucas shook his head and mumbled, "Witches."

Before I even had a chance to get out of the car, the front door to my parents' house opened and my mother, sister, and Lucy all piled out. Sarah screamed, my mother started to cry, and Lucy waved a smudge stick all around me.

"Oh, look at you!" my mother said as she pulled me into her arms. "I'm so glad you're home, Hollie. We've missed you."

I tried to talk, but Lucy had the smudge stick practically shoved up my nose.

"Lucy!" I said, pushing her arm away. "Are you trying to make me throw up with that?"

She looked down at the smudge stick then back to me. "Of course not. I'm simply cleansing all the negativity from traveling away."

I covered my mouth with my hand and stepped away.

"Go put it in the house, Lucy dear," my mother said as she wrapped my arm in hers. "How was the flight over?"

"Long," I replied, watching Lucy dash into the house to place the smudge somewhere I hoped was far away from me. "How come you're not at the store?"

Sarah took my other arm. "Lucy and I decided we needed a day off, and what better reason than celebrating my baby sister and her little munchkin coming back home. Is she kicking a lot?"

"You think it's a girl too?" I asked.

Shrugging, Sarah replied, "I don't know if it is or not. I just said she."

We both turned and looked at my mother. "Don't look at me," she said. "I don't have those kinds of powers."

I frowned. "I feel like it's a girl, but I'm not sure if that's a feeling or a *feeling*. Lucas insists it's a boy, but every now and then I catch him saying *she*. And did I tell you he had a dream that he was holding the baby and could understand her thoughts?"

"No!" Mom and Sarah said at the same time.

"I told you," Mom said. "Lucy said she knew the moment she met Lucas as a young boy that he had the gift of magick."

I slowly shook my head. "I can't believe she never said anything to me."

With a shrug, she replied, "I don't think she ever felt it was her place to say anything."

Once we got into the house, my mother asked, "Would you like something to drink?"

"Lemonade if you have any!" I said hopefully. My mother made the best lemonade with the fresh lemons she grew in her small orchard.

Mom smiled and took my hands in hers. "Of course I have some!" She pulled me in for another hug. "I'm so glad you're back. Have a seat with Sarah and Lucy in the living room, and I'll bring some out along with snacks."

Sarah and Lucy were already sitting down in the living room, their heads bent together as they whispered about something.

When they saw me, they broke apart.

"What was that all about?" I asked.

Sarah rolled her eyes and sighed as Lucy looked up at me and said, "I was telling your sister she needs to talk to you about Matt Merlin."

"Why does that name sound familiar?" I settled into a large arm chair. The baby gave a little kick, and I couldn't help but smile as I rested my hand on my stomach.

"He grew up in Salem and moved away a few years back. He was friends with Lucas."

"That's right!" I said with a laugh. "Didn't you have a crush on him?"

Sarah ignored me and went on. "He showed up one day at the store and went crazy on me. I guess his mother came in one day and bought a potion, and when she showed it to him later, he told her it was all a joke. There was no such thing as magick or special potions, lotions, spells... He went off on us and said we were ripping people off."

"He only has one thing going for him," Lucy said. "He's handsome as all get out."

Rolling her eyes again, Sarah huffed. "If you like the broody, grumpy, self-centered asshole type."

"Language, Sarah," my mother said as she came in with a tray that held a pitcher of lemonade, four glasses, and some cookies she'd made.

"He is!" Sarah stated, crossing her arms over her chest and glaring at the cookies. Dropping her arms to her sides again, she reached for a cookie and nearly ate the whole thing in one bite.

I'd never seen my sister so worked up over a person before. It wasn't like she and Lucy hadn't been confronted over the validity of magickal things before. Why was this particular person getting under her skin? Maybe because it was Matt Merlin. Sarah had been younger, maybe in middle school, when she'd had a crush on him.

"Has he threatened you or the store?" I asked.

Lucy and Sarah shook their heads.

Practically letting out a growl, Sarah stated, "Every time I see him, he stares at me with his judgmental eyes. Drives me insane."

"You don't want to know how many times I've stopped her from putting a spell on him," Lucy said.

"Oh Sarah, you sound like Hollie now."

I jerked my head toward my mother. "Hey!"

Taking a sip of her drink, she smiled and shrugged.

"So, basically he's just annoying?" I said as I set my glass down and took a cookie.

Lucy and Sarah exchanged looks.

"There's more?" I asked.

Sarah stared down at her hands then looked at me. "Interest in witchcraft is the main source of tourism in Salem, and a lot of city leaders know that. Just look at the large number of tourists who come to the town. And we have over five thousand residents who identify as practicing witches."

"You don't have to tell me, Sarah," I said, rolling my eyes. "I ran a business in Salem, so I know what's driving the economy here."

"We haven't had anyone protest magick in years. Some believe in it while some think of it as pure fun," Lucy stated, "but no one outright dismisses it."

I nodded, not really sure where the two of them were going.

"Matt was in the store and picked up one of Sarah's spell kits," Lucy said. "He laughed and told her she was a joke and asked who in their right mind would believe any of this. He called her a con artist."

Gasping, I looked at Sarah. My sister had the sweetest of souls and would do anything for anyone. You didn't even have to believe in magick; she'd help anyone. And her kits truly did help many people, both residents and visitors.

"What made him come back to Salem if he hates it here so much?" I asked.

Mom cleared her throat. "His mother was sick, but she's better now. He was born here and is a direct descendant of Mary Dyer. She was hanged in Boston in 1660, years before the trials. His father has pooh-poohed about witchcraft in the past, but nothing like what his son Matt is doing. Matt's mother, though, seems to be a believer."

"Basically, he's a stick in the mud?" I replied.

All three women laughed, and then my mother replied, "He seems like a nice young man. From what I've heard, he doesn't believe in magick but he knows it's good for Salem's economy."

"So why make waves with Sarah and Lucy?"

Lucy shrugged. "That's what we don't understand. He seems to have more of a problem with Sarah than with me."

I frowned. "Does he have an issue with his mother buying your products?"

"Yes, apparently he does," Sarah replied.

"He hasn't made waves at any of the other stores?" I asked.

Sarah sighed. "Not that I know of."

I stood and started to pace. "Something feels off."

"Told you once she got back she'd pick up on it," Lucy stated.

"What do you mean?" my mother asked.

Turning back to face them, I smiled. "I need to reacquaint myself with Mr. Matt Merlin."

Lucy and Sarah looked at each other then back at me.

"How?" Sarah asked.

"You said he works for the city?" I looked at my mother. Mom nodded. "Yes."

"Well, it just so happens I'm meeting my husband downtown for lunch today. I think I'll snoop around a bit. Maybe stumble into Mr. Merlin."

"The moment he finds out who you are, he's not going to like you," Sarah stated as she crossed her arms over her chest.

With a smile, I replied, "Only one way to find out."

They all exchanged another glance.

Placing my hands on my hips, I looked directly at my sister. "Now, on to my problem. How do I get Lucas to realize he has the gift?"

Chapter Two

Lucas

A knock on my door had me glancing up to see Matt Merlin standing there. He was an old friend who'd lived across the street from me growing up. At one time, me, Matt, and Shawn had been the best of friends. I stood and made my way over to him.

"Matt, it's so great seeing you again. Man, it's been how many years?"

He laughed and shook my hand. "Too many. How have you been? Heard you just got back from Ireland."

Motioning for him to sit down in the opposite chair, I sat behind my desk. "I did, yesterday as a matter of fact. I've been amazing. I'm married and expecting a baby this October."

His eyes went wide. "No kidding? I'm so happy for you. How did you like Ireland?"

"Thank you. Ireland was amazing, but I'm glad to be home. I know my wife, Hollie, is as well. What about you? Married? Kids?"

Laughing, he said, "I've been too busy working."

I leaned back in my chair and asked, "What made you leave Augusta? City planner is an important job, and I thought you loved Maine."

His eyes turned sad. "My mother was diagnosed with cancer some time back, but she's in remission now, thank God. That's the main reason I came back."

"I'm so sorry, Matt. I wasn't aware of that, but I'm glad to hear she's recovering."

He gave me a weak smile. "My dad told me I didn't need to uproot my life because of it. At first I drove back and forth from Maine to Salem, but when Mom was feeling better, they decided to move back to Salem. Ever since then, I've had a strange pull to return as well."

"How long ago was she diagnosed?"

"A year ago. She's doing great, but recently she's been talking more and more about one person in town. She claims this person has helped her in more ways than her doctors ever could. I grew suspicious and came back for a visit a few months ago. Sure enough, that woman owns a store here in Salem."

Curious, I asked, "What kind of store?"

"A witchcraft store."

Oh hell. I know where this is going.

When we were younger, Matt had always teased the kids whose parents practiced Wicca. He never believed in it, and I was pretty sure his skepticism had been passed down from his father and his father before that. It was strange since the entire family was from Salem.

"Why is that a problem?" I asked. "You've lived here long enough to know that it isn't anything new."

He sighed. "It isn't a problem, but I'm worried my mother will fall under the strange spell some of these so-called witches have. They sell bullshit things and market them as spells to help heal or get rid of negative energy."

Narrowing my eyes at him, I asked, "So you don't believe at all that they could possess some sort of magick or gift?"

He laughed. "Gift? Is that what they call it? The magic of pushing their wares on innocent people who want to believe in something like that is the only gift they have. I don't want my mother falling prey to it."

"Has she stopped treatment?"

"No, no, nothing like that. She's done with it since she's in remission."

I leaned forward. "Then why are you worried about it? If it makes her feel better, why not let her believe in it?"

Scrubbing his hand down his face, he sighed. "I don't know what it is, Lucas. Everyone speaks highly of the woman who runs the shop, but when I went in to simply question what she'd sold to my mother, she got all defensive."

Raising a brow, I asked, "Did you simply question her, or did you accuse her of something else?"

He winced. "I might have accused her of ripping people off, but it was only because she got under my skin so much."

I laughed. "Sounds to me like you like her."

Then it dawned on me. Matt had once liked Sarah, Hollie's sister.

"What?" he said with a laugh. "Lucas, we're not ten on the playground anymore. This woman went on the defensive immediately. To me that screams that she's guilty."

"Of what? Selling a product she believes in?"

"No! Of making my mother think some stupid spell is going to help her."

Shrugging, I said, "Maybe you insulted her and she was defending herself, her belief."

He rolled his eyes. "You don't believe in all that hocus pocus bullshit, do you?"

"As a matter of fact, Matt, I do."

Widening his eyes, he dropped back in his chair. "What? How? Why?"

"I've seen it firsthand. The powers of magick."

He let out a humorless laugh then frowned when he saw that I was serious. "How?"

"It's a long story, and one I don't want to get into at work. You should come over for dinner, meet my wife."

Blinking a few times, he groaned. "You married one, didn't you?"

I lifted a brow. "By one, you mean...?"

"A witch? Does she really think she's a witch?"

Nodding, I replied, "And so do I."

Matt's mouth dropped open. "Are you shitting me?"

"Matt, you yourself are a descendant of a so-called witch. Hell, almost everyone in this town is. You really believe that it's all just a marketing trick to get people to come to Salem?"

"I think some of it is. Some folks who own stores in town don't believe in it; they're in it for the profit. Honestly, I do believe that some people around here are pagan. My mother said pagans are in touch with the earth and sky and that they strive to find inner peace. I'm all for that. But when they start making my mother buy their spell kits and crystals and all that shit, then no. I'm not about it."

"But it's fine for all the other people who come to Salem—or who seek it out elsewhere—to believe?"

"Yes. Lucas, I'm just worried about my mother. What if the cancer comes back and she thinks she can fight it with these herbs and shit?"

"First, why are you assuming the cancer will come back? Matt, you need to believe that it won't. That your mother fought it."

He closed his eyes. "I know. I know I should."

"What's the name of the store? I'll ask my wife about the owner and see what she knows. If she doesn't know them, her sister, aunt, or mom will."

I held my breath, already knowing what his answer was going to be.

"The Covens' Magick Cottage."

I stared at Matt. "The Covens' Magick Cottage?"

Matt nodded.

"You're not going to like what I'm about to say."

He frowned. "Do you know the owner?"

I drew in a breath. Matt had been a great friend once upon a time, but Lucy and Sarah were family now. "Yeah, I know them."

"Them?" Matt asked.

With a long exhale, I nodded. "Sarah Craft and Lucy Robbins."

A muscle in Matt's jaw ticked at the mention of Sarah's name. "I wasn't aware both women owned the store."

"Lucy owns it; Sarah simply works for her."

Matt nodded. "Sarah is who I, um, talked to. You kept in contact with her all these years?"

This is going to be interesting.

Smiling, I answered him. "She's my sister-in-law."

Matt's mouth dropped open then quickly shut. He closed his eyes and whispered, "Oh shit."

"Knock knock!" Hollie said as she slipped into my office holding a basket.

I stood and quickly made my way over to her. After kissing her on the lips, I bent over to kiss the baby. "How are you both feeling today?"

"Good. I thought the time difference would mess me up, but I'm actually okay. How's your first day back at work?"

"Interesting," I said as I walked around my desk, signed out of my laptop, and put it in sleep mode. "You ready for our picnic?"

A wide grin appeared on Hollie's face. "I am! Sorry I'm late. I stopped by my mom's, and Sarah and Lucy were there."

"Not at the store?"

"No, they wanted to take the day off since I was back in town. When they found out I was planning on having lunch with you, Sarah decided to head to the store and open it for a half day. Mom and Lucy are enjoying a sister's afternoon together."

"That's nice," I said, putting my hand on Hollie's back and guiding her out of the office.

Hollie flashed me a smile and asked, "Did you have a place in mind for the picnic?"

"How about Forest River Park?"

"Perfect!"

As soon as we got the basket in the car and started to head to the park, I cleared my throat. "An old friend of mine is back living in Salem after being in Maine for the last few years. He was a city planner there."

"Really?" Hollie asked, trying to sound surprised and failing.

"His mother got sick, but she's okay now. His parent's decided to retire here in Salem, and he said it felt like it was calling him to return home."

Hollie jerked her head to look at me. "Is that right?"

I nodded, and when I came to a stoplight, I looked directly at her.

"Hollie, you already know who I'm talking about."

"Do I?"

Sighing, I said, "Matt Merlin. I'm not sure if you remember him from when we were little. He lived across the street from me. Shawn and I were good friends with him."

"I remember him. Sarah said every time she sees him now, he glowers at her. She has no idea why he dislikes her so much other than the fact that she's practicing witchcraft."

When the light turned green, I made a U-turn.

"What are you doing?"

"We need to go talk to Sarah at the store. I think I can clear up why Matt has an issue with Sarah."

"Is it only Sarah? The way she and Lucy made it sound, he has a problem with anything magick."

With a shake of my head, I reached for her hand. "I think it goes deeper than that. I'll explain once we get to the store."

Hollie looked out the window then back in my direction. I could feel her eyes on me. "Sarah liked him when she was younger."

"Did she?" I asked, surprised.

"Yes. She'll deny it, but I'm pretty sure I remember her talking about him. I don't remember him going to school with us, though."

"He never went to school with us. He went to a private school."

"Do you think he actually has an issue with witchcraft or with Sarah?"

Turning to look at Hollie, I smiled. "Oh, I think it has to do with both!"

Hollie laughed. "Oh my gosh, this just got interesting!"

Chapter Three

Hollie

The bell above the door rang as Lucas and I stepped into The Covens' Magick Cottage. Sarah was in the other room with a customer. She glanced over at us, and I held up the basket and pointed to the back. She looked confused but nodded.

Lucas and I made our way back to the office, and I started to take everything out. Thank goodness I had packed a lot for us and there would be plenty of food for Sarah too.

I could hear her finishing up with the customer before she appeared in the door of the office.

"What are you two doing here?"

"Have you eaten lunch?" I asked.

Sarah's gaze bounced from me to Lucas and then back to me. "No."

Smiling, I replied, "Great! Come join us."

Folding her arms over her chest, she narrowed her eyes. "What's going on?"

Lucas reached for a grape and popped it into his mouth, completely leaving it all up to me.

"Matt Merlin."

Sarah pushed off the door. "What about him? Please tell me you didn't put a spell on him— because if anyone's putting one on him, it's me!"

"When in the hell would I have time to do that?" I said. "I was with you, Mom, and Lucy earlier. I mean, I'm getting better at spells, but I'm not *that* good."

Relaxing, Sarah stepped into the office and dropped into a chair. "Sorry. I don't know what's wrong with me. I'm on edge."

"No kidding," Lucas said. When we both turned to look at him, he held up his hands in defense.

"Lucas has something he wants to tell you," I said as I started making up a plate of food.

Sarah looked at Lucas, confused. "What is it?"

"Do you remember Matt from when we were younger?" he asked.

Rolling her eyes, she huffed out, "I remember him. He was jerk then, and he still is."

Clearing his throat, Lucas went on. "I know why he'd been giving you such a hard time."

"What do you know?" Sarah asked Lucas.

He and I exchanged a look. I lifted a brow and motioned for him to answer her.

"Lucas?" Sarah prodded.

After drawing in a breath, Lucas slowly exhaled. "Let me start by explaining why he came after you so hard."

Sarah sat down, and I handed her the plate of food.

"Matt's mother had cancer. She's in remission now, but when Matt found out she was coming to the store and buying some of your potions and spell kits, it scared him."

"Why?" Sarah and I both asked.

"Does he hate magick that much?" Sarah added.

Lucas shook his head. "No, I mean, yes. I don't really know. It's kind of strange. His father is against it and so was his grandfather and his great-grandmother... It's like a family tradition to be against magick."

"But he's a descendant of Mary Dyer," Sarah said, "and she was hanged for being a witch."

Lucas shrugged. "I don't know; he just has a thing about it."

Clearly accepting that answer, Sarah waited for Lucas to go on.

"Matt was worried that his mother would buy into the idea that her health problems could be solved by potions and stones and whatever it was she was buying from you—in place of her medicine or advice from her doctor."

Sarah's eyes went wide. "I would never advise that! She never even mentioned anything about having cancer or needing something to cure it. She wanted something to clear out negative energy in her home. She asked me what natural cleaning products would be healthy to have in the house. She bought the daily shower spell kit that has homemade soap and shampoo in it. She also bought the self-love spell kit that has the after-shower body lotion Lucy makes."

"Oh, I love that stuff!" I added.

Sarah nodded. "The spell inside is harmless."

"You don't have to explain anything to me, Sarah," Lucas said. "I think Matt is scared that if her cancer comes back, she'll turn to you and Lucy for help."

"And I would help her, along with whatever her doctor suggests."

Lucas nodded. "I know you would."

"So little Matty is worried I'm playing doctor? I get it, I do, but that isn't what we're all about!" Sarah stated.

Lucas laughed. "I don't think he'd appreciate you calling him that now. I'm also pretty sure he's acting that way because of the crush he used to have on you."

Closing her eyes, she laughed before looking back at Lucas. "He had a crush on me? I used to have the biggest crush on him, but when I told him he said he could never like a witch."

"I remember that!" I stated as I put my hand on my hip. "I was so mad at him for saying that to you."

"Months after that happened, he asked me to a dance at his private school. I told him I'd rather turn myself into a toad and that he was the last boy I would ever go to a dance with."

"Ouch," I whispered.

Lucas frowned. "Well, now that you understand why he came at you so hard, maybe you should talk to him."

Giving Lucas a look that said he'd lost his mind, Sarah put her plate down and stood. "I am not explaining myself or our shop to that man. He needs to learn for himself; it's not my job to educate him."

"Agreed," I said. "But, maybe he's afraid."

"Of what?" Sarah asked.

The bell above the door rang, and Sarah stiffened.

"What's wrong?" I asked softly.

Snarling up her lip, Sarah turned on her heels. "Speaking of the devil himself."

And with that, she rushed through the office door and back out to the store.

"What was that all about?" Lucas asked.

"Matt's here."

Rolling his eyes, he mumbled, "I'm never going to get used to that."

I got up and went to sneak out when Lucas took my arm. "What are you doing?" he asked.

"Listening, duh!"

"Hollie, you need to let the two of them work this out."

I started to laugh then quickly pressed my mouth shut when Lucas lifted a brow.

"Are you serious?" I asked. "You want me to sit back here and not even listen?"

"Yes. Let your sister handle it."

I folded my arms above my swollen belly. "Aren't you glad to see your friend back in town?"

"Of course I am."

"Aren't you looking forward to spending time with him, you, and Shawn?"

"Yes. The three of us were really good friends once."

I nodded. "Well, if he pisses Sarah off, you better hope he doesn't turn into a frog."

Lucas scoffed. "Please—she can't do that."

The corner of my mouth rose as I sent him a smirk. "And I couldn't help Benny save his pub."

His smile faded. "Point taken. Just be quiet so they don't hear us!"

Lucas and I slipped from the office and went into the back stockroom area. We tiptoed right to the edge of the small hallway that led from the stockroom into the store.

"Sarah, will you look at me, please?"

I couldn't see them, but I assumed that was Matt's voice.

"Okay, are you really going to act like a child and ignore me?" he asked.

"Oh shit," I whispered.

Lucas groaned. "Can she really turn him into a frog?"

I waved for him to be quiet, and we both leaned in closer to hear better.

"I'm sorry, did you need something other than to tell me what an awful person I am?"

"Maybe we can start over. My name is Matt Merlin. You probably don't remember me, but I used to live by Lucas when we were kids."

I would have given anything to see Sarah's face.

"I'm sorry, Mr. Merlin, I don't remember you. Is there anything you need help with?"

"She lied!" I whispered. "Why would she lie?"

There was a bit of silence, and I fought the urge to get down and crawl forward on my hands and knees so I could see what was happening.

Matt chuckled. "You don't remember me?"

"Am I supposed to remember you?" Sarah asked.

"Considering you said I was your first kiss, then yes."

Lucas and I both gasped. He pulled me back, and we looked at each other.

"What?" he whisper-shouted.

My mouth opened and closed about five times before I shrugged. "I had no idea!"

Sarah let out a harsh laugh. "You clearly have me mistaken for someone else. Now, if you don't mind, Mr. Merlin, I have a lot to do, and honestly, I'm not in the mood to be put down by you today."

I heard Sarah moving off to the other side of the store.

"What did you sell my mother?" Matt asked.

"You'll have to ask her."

"You know you're not a doctor."

I screwed up my face. "He messed up."

Lucas nodded. "Big time."

We both stepped out from the stockroom and slowly walked over to the cash register. Sarah had moved into the other room in the store and Matt had followed her. Sarah must have spun around and stopped, because Matt was standing between both rooms and I could see them both.

"Of course I know I'm not a doctor," she said. "I've never claimed to be one. I don't claim to be a healer, either."

Matt let out a small laugh. "You don't honestly think you're a witch, Sarah?"

My sister folded her arms across her chest and glared at him. "Do you remember when you said I kissed like a fish?"

Matt pointed at her. "Ha! You do remember!"

"Do you remember how you got chicken pox the next day?"

Taking a step away from her, Matt laughed. When Sarah didn't return his laughter, he took two more steps away from her.

"That's impossible."

Sarah moved closer to Matt. "Is it? How about we test that theory?"

Lucas clutched at my arm.

"You're crazy," he said. "And my mother isn't thinking clearly, or she'd never have come in here."

I could see Sarah's face harden into pure rage.

"Your mother bought a spell kit for self-love. In the kit was some lotion made by my aunt and a spell."

"What kind of spell?" Matt practically spat out.

"You sit in a comfortable position and surround yourself with the products you use for skin care. The lotion, any powder or face cream, whatever you use that makes you feel pretty or good about yourself. You imagine the products covered in light and pink—maybe gold? Whatever your favorite color is. You slowly run your hands over your body from your feet to your head. As you start to connect with your body, you say the spell."

When she mentioned running your hands over your body, Matt looked her up and down.

Oh my God! He still liked her! I spun around and looked at Lucas.

Lucas nodded. "I know, he likes her."

Pulling my head back, I looked at him. I hadn't said that out loud.

"Then you say*: Love within, love without, I love myself without doubt*. After chanting the spell, you feel the light become part of your body. When that happens, you apply the lotion. After you cover your entire body, you simply say three words."

Matt cleared his throat. "What are those?"

Sarah spoke slowly. "*I. Am. Loved.* You see, your mother told me she was having a hard time connecting with her husband after a recent bout of illness. I never asked what was wrong, but it was clear she was lacking in her own self-love. She simply needed a reminder to love herself—because if you don't love yourself first, how can you let others love you?"

Taking a few more steps away, Matt shook his head. "That's all it was?"

Folding her arms across her chest again, Sarah glared at him. "I believe that in all of us is the power to connect with the earth and the stars. I have a gift, and I use it to help others find that power. Whether you believe in it or not, I'm not here to play God. I'm here to help those who seek my help. If you don't like the way I do it, then you don't have to partake in it. Now, if you'll excuse me, I have a customer."

Matt glanced around the store, but no one besides me and Lucas were standing there. I wasn't even sure Matt saw us. He looked so confused, almost conflicted. There was something in his eyes, but I couldn't read it, which was odd. I was usually good at reading people.

Five seconds later, the bell above the door rang, and without taking her eyes off of Matt, Sarah said, "Good afternoon, Lori!"

Turning to follow Sarah as she approached Lori, Matt looked even more dazed and confused.

"Hello, Sarah. Do you have any of that amazing cream Lucy makes for eczema? It works better than anything I've tried before."

Sarah smiled at Lori and led her away from Matt to the other side of the store. Matt shook his head, glanced around the store, and then made his way to the front door and quietly slipped out. I turned to see Sarah watching him make his escape. As soon as the door to the shop closed, she visibly relaxed.

Lucas took my elbow and led us back to the office. I shut the door then leaned against it while Lucas gave me a questioning look.

"Did you see Matt? He almost looked..."

"Confused?"

Lucas shook his head to correct himself. "No. He almost looked as if he'd had a revelation of some sort."

I drew in a deep breath and slowly exhaled. "The only thing I noticed was how the two of them looked at one another. For a hot second, I swore they were about to kiss!"

Lucas's brows shot up. "That would interesting."

Smiling, I agreed, "It most certainly would be."

"Oh no, Hollie. No. I am not going to let you put a spell on Matt or Sarah."

Putting my hand to my chest as if hurt by his words, I fought back a smile. "Me? I would never do such a thing!"

He rolled his eyes. "Right. And I'm a witch."

I couldn't help but grin.

Chapter Four

Lucas

A week since we'd gotten back from Ireland, Hollie and I stood in the middle of the living room of a house we were looking at. We had both decided to sell our places and buy something big enough to raise a family in, but for the time being, we were living at Hollie's house.

Finding a single-family home in Salem big enough to even think about raising more than two kids in was a task in and of itself.

"Lucas, this place is amazing!" Hollie said, making a turn in the living room for the third time.

Smiling, I nodded.

"Now, you're in the heart of historic Salem," our real estate agent said, "so that's why the price is higher. But this Queen Anne single is so precious that I had to show it to you both."

"JulieAnne, I'm so glad you did! I want to see more!" Hollie exclaimed.

"Let me give you the run-down. The house was built in 1890, and it has four bedrooms, two full baths and two half baths. There's an eat-kitchen, a large family room, and a spacious dining room for hosting dinners. There's also a formal living room, two fireplaces, and the house has the original hardwood floors throughout. It even has a seasonal screened-in porch and a beautiful fenced-in yard—which, I might add, is a rare find this close to downtown Salem."

"You said there was more parking besides the two-car garage?" I asked.

JulieAnne nodded. "Two additional spaces in the driveway, so you have enough parking for a total of four cars."

"It's such a great location, and it ticks off all the things we wanted, besides the three full baths," Hollie said as she looked at me with anticipation in her eyes.

"Let's keep looking at the rest of the house, shall we?" I said.

JulieAnne and Hollie both smiled.

"As you can see, the family room is rather large. There's a large open space above that's used for storage right now. You could easily add in another bedroom and bath."

"That's good to know," I said as we walked into the kitchen.

"It's your typical historical home," she continued. "You don't have the open floor plan, but you could see if you might be able to open this wall so you could look into the family room."

Hollie and I both nodded.

"Here on the other side of the kitchen is the formal living room with another fireplace. There's a small butler's pantry between the living room and the formal dining room."

"Oh, look at that screened-in porch, Lucas!" Hollie exclaimed.

JulieAnne smiled. "There are two staircases, one by the kitchen that used to be for the servants, and the other is right here in the foyer. The only way to get down to the basement is the staircase near the kitchen."

"Let's go down first!" Hollie said.

The basement held the laundry, a large storage area, and a bedroom and half bath. There was plenty of room to turn the half bath into a full bath. It would be the perfect area for a guest room.

"We could turn this large storage area into a man cave maybe!" Hollie stated.

I nodded. "Or another area for the family. A theater room?"

"That's a great idea!" JulieAnne said.

We made up way back up and through the kitchen and to the staircase in the foyer. Upstairs consisted of three bedrooms and two bathrooms. One was in the primary suite.

"I love it. It's so charming," Hollie said.

It still had the original glass windows, beautiful trim work throughout the house, and wood floors that had been well taken care of. The kitchen needed updating, but that could be done when we took down the wall to open it up to the family room.

Hollie jumped up and down a bit. "I think the wood fireplace in the family room is my favorite! No! It's the wood beams across the ceiling."

JulieAnne laughed at Hollie. "If you're looking for an open floor plan, this isn't the house for you. But if you're looking for historical charm, she's the one."

Hollie and I both agreed.

"We'd like to put an offer down," I said.

"The owners are looking to have it closed on as soon as possible. Are you ready to move fast?"

I nodded. "It'll be a cash transaction, so as soon as they can get the title cleared, we're ready to go."

JulieAnne's eyes lit up. "A cash offer? Yes, let's get back to the office right now!"

Hollie tried not to laugh, but did she smile at me and winked. My grandfather had left his house in Boston to me, and I had sold it while Hollie and I were in Ireland. Hollie had also sold her party planning business to Mindy and Joan, her former assistants. With the money we'd made on both, we could purchase the house here in Salem with cash and still make any changes to the house we needed to.

I took Hollie's hand in mine, and we followed JulieAnne out of the house and to our cars.

"Meet you both at the office," she said.

Hollie and I both smiled. Once JulieAnne drove off, Hollie slipped into the car and then started to clap her hands.

"Lucas, it's perfect! The only thing I see that needs updating is that kitchen! It looks like it jumped straight out of the eighties. Plus adding the full bath downstairs and a theater room."

"That can come later. Do you want to take on a house like this? When would we do the kitchen remodel?"

Hollie smiled. "I think we can do it!"

"What if the remodel isn't finished before the baby arrives?"

She thought for a moment, and then her eyes lit up. "We can do it while we live at my house. We assumed we wouldn't be moving out until after the baby came anyway, so it's not that big of a deal."

Smiling, I replied, "Then maybe we can even do the theater room as well!"

Hollie laughed. "Maybe!"

"What do you think?" Tripp asked as we stared down at the

17th century archaeological site that had been discovered when the city was digging to make a parking garage.

"It's a home, no doubt about it. Look at the rock wall here. If we can follow it, we should be able to get the blue-print of the foundation," I replied.

Tripp nodded and bent down. "Is that..."

His voice trailed off and I joined him, staring down at what looked like part of a doll head.

"A doll," we both said in unison.

"Fuck, I love my job!" Tripp stated.

My phone buzzed in my pocket, and I pulled it out to see a text from Hollie.

Hollie: Don't forget about dinner tonight.

Me: I won't. Love you and let me know if you need any-thing.

"Everything alright?" Tripp asked.

"It's all good. And yeah, you can go ahead and get the team over; let's find out what this is."

Tripp looked up at me, confused. "Did I say that out loud?"

"What do you mean?"

Laughing, Tripp shook his head. "It's like you just read my mind. I was about to suggest getting the team over to start excavating around the doll."

I forced a smile. "Great minds think alike."

"I'll say!" Tripp said before he started off to pull a few of the interns away from the foundation wall.

Frowning, I stared down at the exposed doll that had to be least three hundred years old, if not older. I bent down one more time, pulled out my brush, and moved it around the area of the head a bit more. It felt like a bolt of lightning hit me. An old clapboard home with a red door stood before me. I quickly glanced around to see where in the hell I was, but the sound of a door opening had me facing forward once

KELLY ELLIOTT

again. I found myself inside the house, looking at an elaborately carved interior post corbel. Standing next to it was a small girl with blonde hair holding a little doll.

I took a step closer to her, instantly feeling a strong connection between us.

"Does thee know who I am?" she asked, a sweet smile on her face.

Smiling back at her, I shook my head. "I don't. Who are you?"

Hugging her doll to her chest, she giggled. "I'm Charlotte, your daughter."

Stumbling back away from the girl, I tripped over something and fell to the floor.

With a wide grin, Charlotte took a step toward me. "Tis not time yet. You need to wake up now, Daddy."

"Lucas? Lucas? Are you okay?"

The sound of Tripp's voice pulled me from the vision, and I looked up at him. The concern in his eyes caused me to glance around. I was on the ground.

"What happened?" I asked.

"You were standing there, and it looked like you were talking to someone," Hannah, a student intern who was helping with the site, said. "Then you took a step back and tripped, but I'm not sure over what."

"What are you holding in your hand?" Tripp asked.

Glancing down, I found myself staring at a locket. I turned it over and saw the word *Charlotte* etched onto the back. My heart kicked against my chest.

"Where did you get that?" Tripp asked in an amazed voice.

It took me a few moments to reply. I had no fucking idea where I'd gotten it. Not wanting to hand it over as a find from the site, I pushed it into my pocket and replied, "It must have fallen out of my pocket when I fell."

34

"It looks old. What's the story behind it?" Hannah asked.

Forcing a smile, I said, "We'll save that for another time—let's get this doll out, shall we?"

Hannah nodded and moved to the area where the doll was. Tripp gave me a questioning look. "You okay?"

"I'm great. Let's see what we've got here."

The three of us all got down on the ground and carefully worked around the area of the doll. The entire time, I couldn't shake the feeling of déjà vu I kept having.

Chapter Five

Hollie

After setting the lasagna on top of the oven, I slipped the bread in and stood up. I went to turn and stopped when I felt the baby move. Smiling, I put my hand on my stomach.

"Hello, little Charlotte!"

I dropped my hand and stared down at my stomach. "Now why in the world did I just call you Charlotte?"

Another small move. Smiling, I rubbed my swollen belly. "You like that name?"

When the baby kicked, a strange sense of knowing came over me and I startled. I had somehow known that the baby was Charlotte. *She* wanted her name to be Charlotte.

Reaching for my phone, I dialed my mother.

"Hello sweetheart, how's the cooking coming along?" she asked.

"Um, fine. It's great. Mom, I have to ask you something."

"Okay. Ask away."

"When you were pregnant with me and Sarah, did you ever talk to us?"

37

She laughed. "All the time, Hollie. I read to you, sang to you. The baby can hear you."

I drew in a breath. How could I word what I needed to ask without my mother thinking I'd gone insane?

"No, Mom, I mean did you communicate back and forth with us?"

She paused. "No. But I do remember my grandmother saying she could hear my mother's thoughts, but only until she reached a certain point in her pregnancy. Why? Can you hear the baby's thoughts?"

Chewing on my lip, I said, "I'm almost positive she just told me she wants to be named Charlotte."

"Oh, Hollie, sweetheart! That was your third great-grand-mother's name. Or was it your fourth? I can never remember. She was named after her father's sister who passed away when she was young."

"How do you know this?" I asked with a slight laugh.

"It's on the family tree and in the family book. There's a family legend that Charlotte's mother gave her daughter her favorite dolly while she was in labor with her third child. It was a rather difficult birth, and Charlotte had heard her mother crying out and was scared. So, her father gave her the doll and said that Charlotte's mother had asked her to watch over it and practice being a big sister. Sadly, both her mother and the unborn child died in childbirth."

"Mom! That is the saddest thing I've ever heard. Why in the world would you tell me that!"

"Hollie, you're going to be fine. Anyway, Charlotte's fa-ther gave her a locket after her mother passed. On the outside was her name, and on the inside was a picture of her mother."

"Does anyone have the doll or the locket?"

Mom paused for a moment. "Let me see if I remember the story. Charlotte's brother kept a journal, but I cannot for the life of me remember his name. I believe the house burned down with Charlotte and her father inside. Her older brother had gone into town to the market, and he was the only survivor."

I put my hand to my chest. "My goodness, that is heartbreaking."

"It is. But the name is lovely!"

Frowning at the phone, rolled my eyes. Leave it to my mother to put a positive spin on a story like that. I saw Lucas pull into the driveway. "I need to go, Mom. Lucas just got home."

"Okay darling, have a good time tonight, and let's meet for lunch tomorrow."

I smiled even though she couldn't see me. "Sounds good. Bye, Mom."

After hanging up, I rushed over to the door to open it. I could practically feel the negative energy coming off of Lucas.

"Hey, how was your day?" I asked as he stopped to give me a kiss.

"It was...strange."

I shut the door and followed him toward the bedroom.

Lucas sat down on the edge of the bed and stared at me.

"Okay, you're kind of freaking me out," I said. "What's going on?"

He drew in a long breath then exhaled.

"Something happened today, and I don't really know how to explain it. I need a minute to get my thoughts in order." He smiled up at me, but it didn't reach his eyes. "How was your day?"

"It was good, but it must be a day for strange happenings. Do you know how I can sometimes tell what people are going to say before they say it?"

He nodded.

"I think it happened with the baby today."

Lucas's eyes went wide as saucers. "What do you mean?"

"Well, earlier the baby moved and I put my hand on my stomach and said, 'Hello, little Charlotte.' I have no idea why I called her that. She moved again, and I laughed and asked if she liked the name. She kicked hard, and I had the strangest sense come over me. Like déjà vu. It was so strange."

The color drained from Lucas's face.

"Are you okay?"

He slowly shook his head. "Did anything else happen?"

I snarled my lip and sat down on the bench. "Because that isn't strange enough?"

"I'm being serious, Hollie. Did anything else happen?"

With a shake of my head, I replied, "I called my mother to ask if it was possible that I could read the baby's thoughts. I told her what happened, and she said my third or fourth great grandmother was named Charlotte. It was a tragic story, though, and I'm honestly surprised she told it to me."

Lucas leaned forward, looking eager for me to tell him more. "What was the story? Tell me."

I let out a strangled laugh, not sure why he was so intent on hearing this story. "Why? It's kind of sad."

Lucas stood then bent down in front of me. He took my hands in his and said, "Please tell me."

I stared at him in confusion. Why was it so important that I tell him this story? "Um, well, she said Charlotte's mother was in labor with her third child and it was a difficult one. Her father gave Charlotte her mother's favorite dolly to watch over. The mom and baby both died soon after."

"Is that all?" Lucas asked, not sounding at all like himself.

"Ah...um...no. He said..."

"Who said?"

I shook my head, trying to remember the story I had been told mere minutes ago. "Charlotte's brother kept a journal. He, um, wrote that his father gave Charlotte a locket with her name on it and her mother's picture on the inside. I asked about the doll and locket, but my mother said it was most likely lost in a fire."

"Holy shit," Lucas mumbled. "Where was the fire?"

I narrowed my eyes at him, wanting to ask him what was going on. But from the look on his face, I knew he needed me to keep going.

"Charlotte and her father died in their home. Her older brother was in town at the market when it happened."

Lucas fell back onto his ass and started to rock as he whispered, "Holy shit. Holy shit. Holy shit."

Getting down on the floor with him, I pulled at his arm. "Lucas, what's going on? You're scaring me now."

He turned to look at me and then frowned. "You look like her."

"Who?"

"Charlotte," he whispered.

A nervous bubble of laughter came out of my mouth. "Well, we'll find out soon enough."

He shook his head, stood, then helped me up too. "Sit on the bed. I need to tell you something."

I did as he asked and rubbed my hands together nervously. I'd never seen Lucas so rattled. He wasn't even this freaked out when I told him I was a witch. Okay, well, maybe it was a different kind of freaked out.

Lucas paced back and forth before stopping in front of me. "The site that they wanted me to come back and supervise..."

Nodding, I said, "Yes, what about it?"

Clearing his throat, he said, "So far we've dug up part of a foundation of a home. Today, when I was talking to Tripp, we both noticed something in the ground. We both started to look closer and noticed it was doll. Most likely a porcelain doll."

I nodded.

"Tripp went off to get a couple of the interns so we could start working on getting it out. When he left, I bent down to work on the doll and it was like I was transported back to the 1700s. I was a simple clapboard house with a red door. I walked inside and a little girl was standing there."

My heart started to pound. "Was it like a vision?"

He shook his head and paused for a moment. "It was, but at the same time, I knew I was standing in that room, Hollie. I was there. The little girl—she smiled at me and it was the sweetest smile I'd ever seen. She was clutching a doll to her chest, and she asked me if I knew who she was."

Placing my hand on my stomach, I whispered, "Charlotte?"

Lucas swallowed hard. "I asked who she was, Hollie, and she said, 'Charlotte, your daughter.'"

I gasped and placed both hands over my mouth. "Oh my God. Lucas."

Nodding, he said, "I know! That's not even the whole thing."

"Tell me the rest!"

"I was so freaked out I took a few steps away from her. Then I fell—I'm not sure how—but I was just sitting there on the wooden floor of this old home. Charlotte walked up to me and she said..."

His voice trailed off.

"She said what?!" I cried out, causing Lucas to jump.

"Something about how it wasn't time to give it to me yet. Then she said, 'You need to wake up now, Daddy.'"

I was positive my mouth fell to the ground.

"That's not all. Tripp was calling out my name, asking me if I was okay. I got up and Hannah said it looked like I'd been talking to someone, then I took a step back and fell over something that she couldn't see. That's when Tripp asked me what was in my hand."

"What was in your hand?"

Lucas opened his hand to reveal an old locket. I reached for it, and the moment my hand touched it, the baby moved. I jerked my hand away and read the name on it.

Charlotte.

My eyes jerked up and I looked at Lucas. "When I touched it, the baby moved."

He slowly shook his head. "Fucking hell, Hollie. What is going on?"

I stood and smiled. "This isn't bad, Lucas. This just proves I was right! Lucy was right!"

Looking confused, he let out a disbelieving laugh. "This isn't bad? Hollie, what are the odds I'd have this strange vision about a little girl named Charlotte on the same day you called our baby by that very name. We've never even mentioned naming the baby that. And what do you mean you were right? What was Lucy right about?"

Smiling, I took his hand in mine and nearly shouted, "Lucas! You're a witch! Or a warlock, a pagan, or whatever you want to call it. I've had my suspicions since Ireland. This proves it!"

Lucas stared at me, his mouth dropped open and a stunned expression on his face. Then he busted out laughing.

"What's so funny?"

He laughed harder.

"Knock knock!"

The sounds of Kristin's voice calling out from downstairs caused Lucas to laugh even harder.

I spun around to walk away from him. "Ugh! I don't even want to talk to you right now!"

"Wait!" Lucas cried out, bending over as he laughed. "Hollie!"

Storming out of the room, I met Kristin and Shawn in the kitchen.

"What's going on?" Kristin asked as she looked past me toward Lucas.

"My husband is a jackass."

"That's not new news," Shawn stated, popping one of the olives I'd put out earlier into his mouth.

Lucas stood there, attempting to get control of himself. "I'm sorry, I'm sorry. It's just…"

He started laughing again, and that made Shawn laugh.

"Why are you laughing?" Kristin asked.

With a shrug, Shawn laughed harder.

When I saw that Kristin was about to start laughing too, I slammed my hands down on the table. Everyone jumped, including Charlotte—er, the baby.

"There is nothing funny about any of this."

Lucas wiped away his tears. "Actually, there is. Hollie thinks I'm a witch!"

Right at that moment, Sarah walked in. "What?"

All heads turned toward Sarah, and Lucas whispered, "Oh no."

I spun around to look at him. "What do you mean, 'Oh no?'"

Lucas wasn't laughing any longer. When the doorbell rang, Sarah and I both turned toward him.

"What did you do?" Sarah nearly growled.

"I didn't know you'd be here!"

I frowned. "What do you mean you didn't know she'd be here, Lucas? I told you she was coming!"

Lucas closed his eyes and said, "It was a crazy day, Hollie!"

"Tell him to go away!" Sarah shouted.

"God, I've missed family dinners!" Kristin said as Shawn nodded and tossed another olive into his mouth.

I rushed out of the kitchen and to the front door. I didn't need to have powers to know who was on the other side of it. Drawing in a deep breath, I exhaled, put on a smile, and opened the door.

"Matt, I'm so glad you were able to make it to dinner. It's so nice to see you again after all these years!"

He smiled and stepped inside. "Thank you for having me, Hollie. I wasn't sure what to bring, so I brought wine... and these are for you since you can't have the wine."

He produced flowers from behind his back, and I found myself instantly liking the guy. "How sweet of you. Come on in—everyone's in the kitchen."

Matt followed me into the kitchen. I was going to have a long talk with my husband about not telling me who he'd invited over for dinner.

"Lucas, Matt's arrived."

"Hey, Matt," Shawn said as he walked over and shook his hand. "Lucas didn't mention you'd be here!"

Matt smiled and looked at Lucas who just shrugged. When Matt turned to me with a worried expression, I did the only thing I could do to keep him from feeling uncomfortable. "He told me, don't worry."

Kristin snort-laughed then cleared her throat. Shawn introduced Kristin to Matt.

"I don't remember you from school," Kristin stated.

Matt laughed. "I get that a lot. I went to a private school and then we moved to Maine when I was in the seventh grade."

"Oh, okay. What brought you back to Salem?"

I pulled out a vase, put the flowers in it, and walked into the dining room to set them on the table. Sarah stood there with a glare on her face.

"Don't look at me like that!" I said. "I had no idea Lucas asked him over for dinner."

Crossing her arms over her chest, she shot daggers past me at either Lucas or Matt. I wasn't sure which one she was currently madder at.

"I'm leaving!" Sarah hissed.

"You are not. Just give the guy another chance, Sarah."

"Why! He was rude to me, and he clearly doesn't like me."

I let out a small bark of laughter. "Please, the sexual tension between the two of you is off the charts."

Her mouth dropped open. "I'm sorry?"

Leaning in, I lowered my voice. "He was your first kiss, huh?"

She blushed, her cheeks turning pink.

"You liked him!"

She blinked rapidly at me. "When I was thirteen, Hollie!"

I rolled my eyes, grabbed her hand, and pulled her back toward the kitchen. We walked in just as Matt was finishing telling Kristin why he'd moved back to Salem.

"Sarah?" Matt said, his voice a mix of happiness and displeasure.

With a jerk of her head, Sarah replied with a cold, "Matt."

All eyes bounced between my sister and Matt. Clearing my throat, I said, "Lucas, Matt brought a bottle of wine. Why don't you have everyone go take a seat and pour them a glass while I get everything ready?"

As everyone made their way out of the kitchen, I took hold of Kristin and pulled her to me. In a low voice, I said, "We need to talk."

"About?" she asked, one brow raised in question.

"I need your help with a spell."

Her eyes lit up. "If it's to get Matt and Sarah together, I'm all over it!"

"No!" I said, angry with myself that I hadn't made that spell yet. "It's for Lucas."

Kristin took a step back. "The last spell you put on him nearly killed him!"

"I'm a better witch now!" I said as I turned to take the bread out of the oven.

Folding her arms over her chest, she scoffed. "Oh, from all the years of practice. Oh wait, it hasn't even been a year yet."

I gave her a slight push toward the dining room. "Go make sure Matt and Sarah don't kill each other."

She pouted. "You really are no fun now that you're pregnant."

Pointing to the dining room, I growled, "Kristin!"

She lifted her hands in surrender. "Fine. But I don't know when I became the babysitter around here."

Chapter Six

Lucas

Dinner was lovely. Well, it was lovely as long as Matt and Sarah ignored each other. Lucas still seemed a bit off kilter, though. I couldn't believe what had happened to him, and I was dying to talk to Lucy about it. I'd sent her a voice text earlier when I'd left the table with the excuse of needing to use the bathroom.

I knew some witches had precognitions—the ability to see into the future. But it usually only lasted for a few seconds. Sarah had it, there was no doubt about that. But could a witch travel back in time?

Glancing up, I saw Lucy at the back door of my house. She smiled, and I nearly dropped the dessert I was about to bring out to everyone. I rushed over to her. "Give me one second!"

Softly shutting the door, I made my way to the dining room and motioned for Kristin to come into the kitchen. She rose and quickly made her way toward me.

"What's up?"

Handing her the dessert, I said, "I need you to serve this and tell everyone I had to go to the bathroom."

Her brow rose. "Again?"

"I'm pregnant, Kristin. I have to pee a lot."

She shot me a look that said I was full of bullshit. "And the fact that Lucy is waiting for you outside has nothing to do with this?"

My eyes widened. "Omg! Your gifts are growing stronger!"

She shook her head. "Not really; I can see her pacing on the back porch."

I glanced over my shoulder and frowned when I saw my aunt doing just that.

"Go, I'll stall for you."

"Thanks!" I said, kissing Kristin on the cheek and making my way out to Lucy.

Once I was outside, she took my hand and we walked into the small backyard.

"Did you get my message?" I shook my head. "Of course you did, you're here. Can Lucas time travel?"

Lucy smiled. "It sounds like Lucas stumbled into a time hole."

"A what?"

"It's a space between the present and the past. Not everyone can see them, and most often a witch falls into one when someone from their past needs them to know something."

"Lucy, is this baby I'm carrying our great, great, great... whatever grandmother?"

Taking my hand in hers, Lucy said, "I do believe you are carrying the reincarnation of Catherine. Her life was taken so early on."

"Why has she waited so long to find a new beginning?"

Lucy shrugged. "Maybe she hasn't. I'm going to guess her mother had the gift, and Catherine may have had it as well. Her brother did."

My brows shut up. "He did?"

She nodded.

"Why did Lucas find the hole and not me if we're distant relatives?"

Lucy looked over my shoulder then turned to stare directly into my eyes. "Because Lucas has the gift."

"I knew it! Sarah said you knew it as well. Why haven't you ever told me?"

"Because a witch has to find their gift on their own."

Pouting, I said, "What's the fun in that?"

She brought her hands to her hips. "Hollie, do not use an unbinding spell on him."

I gasped. "What's that? Oh my goodness, is there a spell to make him realize he's a witch?"

Closing her eyes, Lucy whispered, "Oh dear."

She looked back at me and sighed. "You said Lucas has the locket?"

"Yes, he said it appeared in his hand."

"No, he conjured it without even knowing it."

"From where?" I asked in shock.

"The homestead. There's a reason Lucas was called back to that site. He's meant to be the one who uncovers it. As soon as the two of you got married, it started this whole thing."

"With Charlotte?"

She nodded. "I'm not sure why. I'll need to do some digging into Lucas's family history as well."

"Does one of his parents have the gift?"

Lucy shook her head. "I don't think so. It can skip generations. I'll start working on it today—and I'll look for Matthew's journal too."

The door opened, and Sarah stepped out.

"I'll help."

I smiled at my sister. She'd clearly had a vision about this conversation.

"You two girls—the powers you have are something else," Lucy stated with a smile. "Go back in now. I'll keep you updated."

After we each hugged and kissed Lucy, I quickly filled Sarah in on what happened to Lucas. She stood there, stunned.

"I know. It's crazy, right? I mean—" I put my hands on my stomach. "This could be Charlotte. Do you think she'll remember anything from her previous life?"

"I've read a lot of stories about people remembering bits and pieces of their previous life. There was a little boy who started having nightmares when he was two, I think. In his previous life, he'd been a World War II pilot."

"Wow."

"Excuse me! Why are you both out here without me?" Kristin said as she opened the back door and walked toward us. I wasn't entirely ready to tell her what had happened with Lucas just yet, but now that I had both my sister and Kristin here, I needed their help.

"I need to do an unbinding spell," I blurted out.

"Oh my God, no!" Sarah started to walk away.

"For what?" Kristin asked with a bubble of excitement in her voice.

I drew in a breath. "I need Lucas to realize he has the gift."

"Count me in!" Kristin said without so much as batting an eye.

I turned to my sister, but she shook her head. "No. And I cannot believe Lucy told you that you needed three members of a coven to do it."

My brows shot up. "She didn't, but thank you for that information."

"No. I'm not doing it."

I reached for her hands. "Sarah, please."

She looked at Kristin who shrugged. "I mean, with you here, what could go wrong?"

Pointing to me, Sarah said, "It's Hollie we're talking about."

Kristin grinned. "Touché."

Sarah turned to me. "Hollie, if he really does have the gift, it will reveal itself in time."

"I've been waiting, but he keeps ignoring all the signs. Even today, he laughed when I mentioned it. Please, Sarah! Pretty please with a cherry on top!"

I gave her my best pouty face, and she closed her eyes and slowly shook her head.

"I am so going to regret this."

I placed my hands on her arms and smiled at her. "I promise you, you won't regret it!"

Kristin laughed. "Famous last words."

The next day found me, Kristin, and Sarah at The Covens' Magick Cottage. Sarah held up a bottle of Moondust.

"What's in it?" Kristin asked.

"Sea salt," I said as I took the bottle. "Because of the connection between the sea and the moon. Jasmine ashes, because jasmine corresponds with the moon. Glitter because it reflects light, just like the moon. I made it last night and Sarah charged in the moonlight overnight."

Nodding like she understood, Kristin looked from the bottle to me and then asked, "What's the connection with the moon?"

"It's used to call energy from the moon for the spell," Sarah stated like Kristin should have known that. "Are you not reading the book I gave you?"

Rolling her eyes, Kristin said, "I'm trying to, but I keep falling asleep!"

I couldn't help but giggle. Taking Kristin's arm, I said, "Come on, let's go."

"I can't believe I'm doing this," Sarah grumbled before she asked, "You have everything else?"

Smiling, I said, "Yep, got it all.

Sarah could pretend she didn't want to do this, but I knew she was as curious as I was.

The three of us made our way toward Midtown Park. I wanted to do it at the park since it was close to both Lucas's job and the dig site, and I wasn't sure where he would be during the time of the spell.

"I really hope no one knows what we're doing." Kristin glanced around while putting down the blanket.

Sarah scoffed. "Why? Because we live in a town where every other person practices magick?"

Kristin brought her hands to her hips. "People expect it from you two. They don't expect it from me!"

I sat down next to Sarah, and we started to lay everything out.

"What's the bowl for?" Kristin asked.

"To grind everything together. Will you pick that dandelion flower for me? But don't do anything to it yet," I stated.

Kristin leaned over and picked the flower. "This has to be the biggest dandelion I've ever seen."

Sarah laughed. "It is! I've never seen one so big."

After I had everything laid out, we sat in a circle.

I closed my eyes and thought of Lucas. When I opened my eyes, Kristin was glancing between me and Sarah.

"Was I supposed to be doing anything?"

I smiled and shook my head. With a deep breath, I asked, "Ready?"

"So ready!" Kristin said.

"I hope you know what you're doing, Hollie," Sarah whispered.

I started to hum in a low voice, and Kristin and Sarah joined in as we all held hands. I dropped Kristin's hand and started the spell.

Pouring the moondust into the bowl, I said, *"A bit of moondust, a must. A sprig of hair gotten on a dare."*

Kristin had managed to pull a few strands out of Lucas's hair last night, much to his dislike.

"Add a pinch of sage spice to make everything nice."

I dropped the spice into the bowl with the few hairs and the moondust.

"Grind it into the finest powder and sprinkle on a dandelion flower."

As I ground the ingredients into a fine powder, Sarah squeezed my left hand.

Kristin held up the flower up over the bowl while I sprinkled it over the top.

Holding the flower up, I said, *"Blow into the wind and let his binded powers rescind!"*

Turning to Sarah, I chuckled. "Will you help me blow it? It's so big."

She winked. "Let's do this."

We both drew in a breath and blew. The three of us watched the dandelion fluff float into the air.

"Now we sit back and wait and see," Kristin stated.

Sarah chewed nervously on her thumbnail.

"Were we supposed to think about Lucas at all?" Kristin asked.

When we both turned to look at Sarah, she swallowed. "I hope not."

"Don't worry, I was!" I said as I watched Sarah's cheeks turn bright pink.

Chapter Seven

Lucas

Matt and I walked out of Nathaniel's Restaurant and started toward The Common, a local park, since cutting through it would bring us back to the office sooner. I needed to check my emails before I headed back out to the dig site.

A gust of wind hit and pollen flew into our faces.

"Shit, that got in my mouth!" Matt started to make sounds with his mouth like he was spitting something out.

I blinked a few times and waved the air in front of my face. "Where did that gust of wind come from?" I asked, laughing.

"What in the hell!" Matt called out before he sneezed. A woman walking past us let out a little yelp as her blouse ripped open like an invisible hand had pulled it apart.

Matt and I stood there, stunned.

"Ma'am, your shirt," Matt stating, pointing at her.

She glanced down and let out a yelp and started to quickly pull her shirt together as she practically ran away.

Matt and I both looked at each other.

"That was weird," I said on a laugh.

"It sure was."

We made our way through the park, and once we got back to the city offices, Matt stopped. "Do you hear that?"

"Hear what?"

He looked around then started to turn in a circle.

"Matt?"

"You don't hear that high-pitched sound?"

I focused on listening. "I don't hear anything."

"It sounds like laughter."

Reaching into my pocket, I said, "Hold on, I need to take this call."

It wasn't until I was staring down at my phone in my hand that I realized it wasn't ringing. When it did, I jumped, nearly dropping the phone.

"What in the hell?"

I answered the phone and cautiously said, "Hello?"

"Lucas, it's Hannah from the Gable's dig."

"Oh, hey Hannah, what's going on?"

"We have the doll out."

My eyes widened. "I'm on my way."

I hung up and looked at Matt. "I need to go. They got the doll out."

He straightened. "Hey, can I come? I don't have any meetings for the rest of the afternoon. I'd love to see an actual dig site."

"Sure, come on. I need to get there quickly."

The drive to the site only took a few minutes. The house was on the outside border of modern Salem. During the short drive, I couldn't stop thinking about how I'd known my phone was about to ring. Ever since I'd married Hollie, the strangest things had been happening to me. Now it seemed like I could sense something before it even happened.

Hollie's words from dinner replayed in my mind. A witch? There was no way. Or was there?

"I could go for an apple pie," Matt randomly said. "I just got a legit craving for it."

Laughing, I pulled in and parked. "Stop at Salem Pie House and get one on the way home."

He nodded. "I might do that."

"Remember, don't touch anything while you're here."

"I won't."

As we walked toward the site, I noticed someone sitting at a table nearby.

"Would either of you be interested in an apple pie?" the woman asked with a smile. "We're having a bakery fundraiser for the Salem Witch Museum."

Matt nearly sprinted over to her. "I was just telling my friend I wanted apple pie!"

She smiled up at him and slid him a piece that was wrapped in plastic.

Matt gave her a twenty. "Keep the change since it's for a good cause."

I frowned while he made his way back over to me, removing the wrapper and picking up the pie as he walked. He took a large bite, closed his eyes, and moaned in delight.

"Good?" I asked.

"Best apple pie of my life."

"You do realize you just donated to the Salem Witch Museum, Matt, don't you?"

He paused a moment then said, "It's still part of our history, right?"

Rolling my eyes, I started back toward the site. As soon as I got there, I saw a group of people bending over to look at what I assumed was the doll.

"Tripp," I called out, causing him to look up.

A wide smile played across his face. "You've got to see this, Lucas."

A few people parted and I stared down at the doll. It looked almost perfectly preserved.

"How is it in such good shape, Lucas?" Hannah asked.

"Was it wrapped in anything?" I asked as I examined the venetian doll.

Tripp nodded and said, "It appears it was wrapped in a blanket, though only bits of the fabric were still intact under the doll."

"The crazy part is that nothing was broken. How do we have a two to three-hundred-year-old porcelain doll that was buried in a burnt-down home still in near-perfect condition? The hair wasn't even burned," Tripp stated.

We all stood there, staring down at it.

I looked up and glanced around before looking at Tripp. "I saw its hair yesterday as well as the side of the face. I knew it would be in decent shape, but this is crazy."

Matt leaned over and looked down at the doll too. "That doll looks familiar."

All eyes turned to Matt.

"What do you mean?" Tripp asked.

"I've seen it in an old picture, though I can't place where." He looked up from the doll and shrugged. "Man, it's hot. We could use some rain."

Before I could even say a word, someone walked by carrying a bucket of water to clean off any artifacts that were found. The guy tripped, and the entire bucket of water went flying right towards Matt and drenched him.

Hannah gasped, as did a few other people, while Tripp laughed. "Bet you're not hot now," he said.

Matt looked at Tripp and slowly shook his head.

"Get this bagged up before anything happens to it. Has it been cataloged?" I asked.

Someone from the back of the group confirmed that it had.

Turning to Tripp, I asked, "Anything else?"

"We covered the site up; weather's calling for some rain."

I nodded and glanced back at the area. A group was in the process of putting a tent over the site now that we had most of the foundation exposed. "I want to focus back on the wall once the rain passes. I'm going back to the office to see what I can find out about this house."

I stopped and looked back at Tripp. "How do you know the house burnt down?"

"We found some charred wood, and the rocks on the foundation indicate a fire as well."

Nodding, I said, "If you come across anything else, call me."

"Sounds good. I'll let you know when we open the site back up."

After one look at Matt, I exhaled. "Let's find a towel or something before you get into my car soaking wet."

Two hours later, I sat in my office and poured over old records in an attempt to figure out who that house might have belonged to. I knew Charlotte had lived there, but was this the house Hollie and her mother had been talking about? The one that had burned down with Charlotte and her father still inside of it?

A knock on my door caused me to look up. I saw Matt standing there with a strange expression on his face.

"What's wrong?" I said.

"I need to talk to you."

Standing as well, I motioned for him to come in. He shut the door and made his way over to me. He had changed since we'd visited the dig site and was now wearing slacks and a polo shirt.

"What's going on?" I asked.

He drew in a deep breath and then laughed on the exhale. "You're going to think I'm crazy."

It was my turn to laugh. "Try me."

He rubbed his hand on the back of his neck as he looked down at the floor and then back up at me. "I think Sarah put a hex on me or something."

My brows shut up in surprise. "Why do you think that?"

"Ever since we walked out of that restaurant earlier and that gust of wind hit us, shit has been happening to me."

"Describe shit."

"Okay, well, that lady whose shirt just happened to pop open... I actually went out on a date with her a few weeks ago. I liked her, but not enough for a second date. I saw her in the restaurant and for a fleeting moment as we were leaving, I found myself wondering what her breasts looked like."

"Why were you wondering that?"

"I saw her getting up to leave and...well, fuck, Lucas, I'm a guy!"

I held up my hands. "Fair enough."

"You don't find it strange that I wanted to see her breasts and then a minute later they're in my face?"

"Not really."

He sighed. "The apple pie?"

"Okay, I will admit that was a crazy coincidence."

"The water bucket?"

I laughed. "That was simply bad luck."

He rolled his eyes and started to pace in front of me. "I went home and changed and then came back here. I decided to walk to the office, and for some stupid reason Sarah popped into my head and I stupidly wished I could see her. Not five seconds later, she came out of a store and we ran into each other. And she gasped when she looked at me. Then she said something off-the-wall weird."

"What did she say?" I asked.

"She lifted her hand and pulled something out of my hair. Then she mentioned something about a dandelion."

I frowned.

"That's not the worse of it."

Crossing my ankles as I leaned on my desk, I said, "Go on."

"In my mind...*in my mind*, Lucas, I wanted her to kiss me. Suddenly she walked to me, lifted up on her toes, and planted a kiss right on my lips. Then she jumped back and shook her head. She touched her lips and accused me of kissing her! Me, kissing her! She was the one who kissed me!"

It was hard not to smile. "Did you enjoy it?"

"Did I enjoy it? That's what you're asking me? Maybe you should ask why everything I've been wishing for is coming true!"

I shrugged. "It's your lucky day, maybe?"

"No, it was very clear to me that Sarah didn't want to kiss me. She turned and practically ran away."

"Matt, I think you've had a long day and you're over-thinking everything."

Someone knocked on my office door.

"Come on in!" I called out.

Maxwell Cash walked in and smiled at Matt. "Here you are, Matt. I've been looking everywhere for you. I have some news for you. Good news."

Matt slowly stood and whispered, "Oh no."

"Lewis Harding has stepped down as Assistant City Manager, and Frank would like to offer you the job."

I pushed off my desk and reached for Matt's hand to shake it. He stood there dumbfounded.

"Look at that, Lucas," Maxwell said. "He's so happy he can't even speak."

"Something like that." I watched all the color drain from Matt's face.

Giving Matt a hard pat on the shoulder, Maxwell said, "Come to my office first thing tomorrow, and I'll go over everything. Then you can decide if you want to officially take the job."

With a wave in my direction, Maxwell swept out of my office. Matt turned to face me and then stood frozen in place.

"Let me guess," I said, "you wished you could get the Assistant City Manager job?"

Looking like he might faint, Matt stumbled over to the small sofa in my office and sat down. He buried his head in his hands and mumbled something.

"What was that?" I asked.

Looking up at me, he repeated his words. "I'm afraid to think."

"You're afraid to think? Matt, I think you're over-thinking this."

He shook his head, a look of panic in his eyes.

"What in the hell do I do now, Lucas?"

I drew in a deep breath and exhaled. "I think we need to talk to Hollie."

"Hollie? Will she be able to tell if someone put a hex on me?"

I clenched my jaw tightly together to keep from saying that I had a feeling Hollie was the one who had a hand in this, and I gave him a nod.

Matt rushed to the door. "Then let's go!"

I glanced at my desk then back at Matt. "Give me a few minutes to get things wrapped up here, and then I can meet you at my house."

"No, no, I can't drive. I can't trust myself to do anything!"

I stared at him, fighting the urge to walk over and slap the sense back into him and yell that he needed to get his shit together. Instead, I gave him another nod. "I'll come get you when I'm ready to leave."

As I watched Matt leave my office and shut the door, I rounded my desk and picked up my phone.

"Hey!" Hollie said after it only rang once. "How's it going?"

She was way too chipper.

"Hollie, what did you do?"

"Do? Why? Do you feel...different? Ready to admit that you have the gift?"

I paused. Looking at my closed office door, I shut my eyes and sighed. "Oh holy hell."

Chapter Eight

Hollie

The tone of Lucas's voice was lower than normal—a clear indication that he knew I'd put a spell on him. I ignored the million questions I wanted to ask him. Did he feel different? Had he noticed it right away? Was he ready to admit the truth?

"Hollie, I'm bringing Matt home for dinner."

Frowning, I said, "Matt? Okay. But I thought you wanted to plan out what we were going to grill for the Fourth of July party."

"I do. We will. I've got a lot to talk to you about, so I'm leaving now. See you in a bit."

Something was wrong. Very wrong. *Shit. Shit. Shit.*

"Okay, I love you. Be careful driving."

"Love you too."

The call ended, and I looked over at Lucy, Sarah, and my mother. Sarah clearly saw the worry on my face, because she said, "Well?"

Lucy and Mom exchanged a look. It hadn't taken Lucy or my mother long to piece together the one-sided conversation—plus I was sure the covert glances between Sarah and I weren't helping.

"You didn't," Lucy said. Turning to look at Sarah, she asked, "You helped her?"

"I had to! I was also curious to see if Lucas has the gift!" Sarah stated.

Lucy closed her eyes and my mother sighed.

"Let me guess, something went wrong?" Lucy asked.

I wrung my hands together. "I'm not sure. Lucas didn't seem very happy, and he said he was bringing Matt over here."

"Matt?" Sarah asked. "Why?"

"I don't know, but when he asked that stupid dreaded question...*what did you do*," I said in a lowered voice, "I had a feeling he wasn't talking about himself."

Sarah gasped and put her hand to her mouth. We all turned to look at her.

"What is it?" I asked.

"A few hours after the three of us cast the spell today, I ran into Matt. As we were talking, I had this strange, out-of-body experience. Something told me to kiss him, and I did. It was like I couldn't even control myself. How scary is that?" Sarah said with a nervous laugh.

"You wanted the kiss," Mom said while Lucy nodded.

"What?" Sarah let out another bubble of something that sounded more like a moan than a laugh. "Don't be ridiculous."

My mother crossed her arms over her front and gave my sister a knowing look. "No one has the power to make another person do something they don't want to do by using magick. You know this better than anyone, Sarah."

"Mom, are you saying I *wanted* to kiss Matt and made myself do it?"

Mom and Lucy exchanged a look. "It sounds to me like it was Matt who wanted it," Mom said. "He wished it, and you wanted to do it—so there you go."

Sarah shot her gaze over to me. "Did we use the wrong hair?"

"Wait, I'm so confused. So if Matt wished it and Sarah wanted it, then it made it happen?" I asked.

Lucy nodded. "Clearly, Sarah must have been thinking about someone entirely different when you cast the spell."

"No, that can't be! We used Lucas's hair. Kristin said she got hair from Lucas, not Matt."

"Wait, Kristin was involved? She wasn't part of the spell, was she?" Lucy asked.

"Yes," I state. "Sarah said we needed three witches. It was me, Kristin, and Sarah."

The moment I spoke the words, the three of them all looked down at my swollen belly.

I took a few steps back and pressed my hand to my stomach. The baby decided to kick at that very moment.

"It was four of you!" Mom exclaimed.

Sarah closed her eyes. "And we used moondust."

My mother gasped. "Oh my gosh."

Lucy waved her hands around to get everyone to call down. "Okay, well, let's not panic until we know what's happening."

Mom walked over to the teapot, picked it up, and filled it with water. "I'll get some tea going. Meanwhile, get Kristin over here. We need to make sure she actually stole Lucas's hair and not Matt's."

I gasped. "Wait, does this mean Matt is..."

My words faded as I looked around at the three women. Mom smiled, Lucy looked worried, and Sarah looked sick to her stomach.

"He hates witches," Sarah whispered before dropping down into a chair at the breakfast table. "He's going to kill me."

Lucas called out to signal he was home, and the five us all jumped up and rushed into the living room. Standing next to Lucas was Matt. He had a strange, dreamy look on his face, and when he saw Sarah, his eyes lit up.

Sarah clutched my arm and whispered, "Oh God! Oh God."

"What?" I whispered back.

"He wants to do a lot more than kiss!" Sarah stated.

I turned to look at her and smirked. "Well, clearly from your reaction just now, so do you."

Glaring at me, she pushed me forward until I was standing in front of her.

"Well, if the gang isn't all here," Lucas said, dropping his keys in the bowl by the door and giving each of us a pointed look.

"He seems the same," Kristin said as she slowly shook her head. Then she covered her mouth with her hand. "You have the same color hair as Matt."

I closed my eyes and moaned. "You had one job, Kristin! One! Job!"

"In my defense," my best friend said, her hands on her hips, "I was trying to go fast, and I was standing behind him at the time. Look at the two of them. They have the same build! The same hair. It was an honest mistake. Oh, but wait."

Turning to look at her, I asked, "What?"

Kristin chewed on thumbnail then dropped her hand. "Well, I didn't think one strand was enough, so I snuck back in and got another strand, and I might have taken one from each of them."

I looked at Lucas. "You don't feel any different?"

He narrowed his eyes and focused on me. Then, as if a lightbulb went off, he slowly shook his head and scrubbed his face with his hand.

"Yes, Matt!" Lucas snapped.

Matt looked confused. "Yes to what? I didn't ask you anything."

Lucas jerked his head and looked at me. I couldn't help but smile.

"The visions?" he said.

I nodded.

"I thought I was just imagining that I was sensing things before they happened."

With a shake of my head, I smiled. "Welcome to the co-ven."

Lucas closed his eyes and drew in a few deep breaths.

"That poor child doesn't stand a chance if both of her parents are witches," Kristin said with a giggle.

"Are you ready to admit it yet?" I asked Lucas.

He simply sighed in defeat—but he still hadn't admitted it.

"Okay, so while we wait to see if the spell worked on Lucas, what's going on with this one?" Kristin asked.

We all turned to look at Matt. He was holding a pencil and moving it in a circulation motion. "I command you to turn into a toad!"

I followed Matt's gaze and had to cover my mouth when I realized he was trying to turn the key bowl into a toad.

He squeezed his eyes shut and said, "I could really go for some pizza."

"I hope you made pizza," Lucas said.

"She made enchiladas," Lucy responded.

"That really stinks; doesn't pizza sound good right about now?" Matt asked as Sarah let out a sigh of frustration.

"We don't have pizza, Matt!"

The doorbell suddenly rang, and Matt opened it. A young boy wearing a T-shirt that said *Mario's Pizza* stood there looking confused.

"Um, I don't know why I'm here—maybe I got the address wrong. Did you guys order pizza?"

Matt grinned. "Pay the man, Lucas!" He took the three boxes of pizza out of the boy's hands and headed toward the dining room. Lucas glared at Matt as he walked to the door and asked the kid how much we owed.

Lucy, Mom, and Kristin all followed Matt into the dining room while Kristin declared that if there was pepperoni and mushrooms, she wanted a piece.

"What about the dinner I made?" I asked.

Kristin gave me a one-shoulder shrug. "It's Mario's, Hollie!"

I rolled my eyes and watched Lucas walk up to us.

"That's been happening all day," he said. "A woman's blouse just popped open in front of us and gave Matt a clear view of her chest after he wondered what her breasts looked like."

Sarah snarled her lip.

"Then he said he was in the mood for apple pie, and next thing you know, we find a lady who's selling apple pie slices for a fundraiser. He said he was hot and wished it would rain, and then a bucket of water got spilled on him. He wished Sarah would kiss him, and from what he said..."

She nodded. "I did."

"But Lucy said Matt can't control people like that. They have to want it."

Lucas raised his brows and smiled at my sister.

"Don't even, Lucas!" Sarah warned.

He held up his hands in a show of defeat and chuckled.

"Did anything else happen?" I asked.

"He got a position at work he was hoping to get."

Sarah and I exchanged a look.

Lucas eyed us both. "Do either of you want to tell me what in the hell is going on? Because he seems to be getting worse. He told me earlier that he doesn't even want to think because he's so afraid something will happen."

Sarah frowned. "Well, he's right to a certain extent. Some of it might have simply been a coincidence."

"Okay, but how did this happen?" Lucas asked, looking at me.

Screwing up my face, I replied, "Well...um...you see...for the last few months, you've been showing signs."

He sighed. "Hollie, I'm nahhh. I'm nahhh..."

Narrowing my eyes, I asked him, "What are you trying to say?"

"I can't say it. I'm nahhh. What in the hell!"

Sarah started to laugh. "Oh my God. The spell made it so you can't deny the truth!"

Lucas looked at her then at me. "You did cast a spell on me? Again!?"

I rolled my eyes. "Of course I did! It's me! Do you not know me at all?"

"As much as you want to deny it, Lucas, you can't," Sarah said. "You've got the gift of magick, my sweet brother-in-law."

Lucas stumbled back, and I went to reach for him. He shook his head and righted himself. With a sigh, he scrubbed his hand down his face and looked directly at me. "My granny told me when I was younger that I was special. That I had magick flowing through my veins."

My mouth gaped open. "And you didn't think to tell me that?"

73

He looked exasperated. "Hollie, I was like ten! I thought she meant I was her favorite grandson or that I could do anything if I put my mind to—that kind of magic. Not *the* magick. It wasn't until we got together that I started to notice things happening."

Sarah and I both leaned toward him. "What kind of things?" we asked in unison.

Lucas shrugged. "First, it was this weird intuition. I don't know how to explain it. It's especially strong during a full moon."

"Go on!" Sarah urged.

"A few months back, my mom said she wasn't feeling well. She had the flu. I told her to make chicken soup, but that it had to be homemade. And that while she was cooking it, she needed to repeat the words: *Cold, flu, chills be gone. Nothing but a healthy body from now on.* At the time, I simply thought it was because all of Hollie's rhymes had rubbed off on me. Mom thought it was a spell from Hollie, so she did it, and the next day she felt better and the day after that she was back to normal."

I gasped. "You cast a spell! Holy crap, Lucas Payton, you cast a spell and you didn't tell me!"

"I thought it was a fluke!"

Turning to look at Sarah, I laughed. "He cast a spell!"

"And it worked." She pointed toward Lucas with a jerk of her thumb and said, "Can you teach her that trick?"

"Hey!" I said as Lucas tried not to laugh.

Sarah walked over to him. "You know why you can't say that you're not a witch?"

Closing his eyes, Lucas nodded. "I can't say them because I'm..."

I held my breath and waited.

"You're?" Sarah probed.

He snapped his eyes open and nearly yelled, "Because I'm a witch!"

At that moment, Matt walked in and let out a scream that sounded like someone had stepped on a cat.

"Noooo, Lucas, no! Not you too!" He dropped his head and said, "I need a hug."

And just like that, Sarah and I both walked up and hugged him. I jumped back as Sarah pushed Matt away.

"Stop wishing for things, jackass!" she shouted.

"I can't help it!" Matt exclaimed.

"You know what needs to be done," Lucas stated, and all our eyes fixed on him.

Sarah shook her head. "No."

Clearing my throat, I replied, "I think he's right."

My sister spun around and glared at me. "No!"

With a nod, I looked at Matt. "You need to take him home and keep an eye on him."

"Me!" Sarah shrieked as Matt perked up.

Attempting not to laugh, I added, "I think it's for the best!"

Sarah pointed at Matt and said, "You be quiet! This has nothing to do with you!"

Matt's eyes went wide.

"Take him home, Sarah. Elaine and I will gather everything we need," Aunt Lucy said as she walked into the kitchen with my mother.

"What about me? Do you need me?" I asked.

"No!" everyone in the room shouted. Well, everyone except Matt.

I folded my arms and huffed.

My mother walked over to me while Sarah grabbed Matt and practically dragged him out of the kitchen, Lucy following behind.

"Hollie, sweetheart. Out of all of us, you're the one with the most power behind your spells, and now that you're pregnant, well, your spells are getting a little bumpy."

"A little?" Lucas asked with a laugh. When I glared at him, he pressed his mouth together lightly.

"Now, Lucas has something he needs to talk to you about," Mom said. "I'll check in with you later."

We both watched my mother whisk out of the kitchen. Turning to look at me, Lucas drew his brows together. "I didn't think your mom could read minds."

I gave him a wink. "It's the mom intuition."

Chapter Nine

Lucas

I stared at the locket in my hand and rubbed my thumb over the engraved name on the back. The memory of the vision came back to me, and I closed my eyes, almost willing myself to go back in time. When nothing happened, I scoffed.

"Magick my ass."

As I stood to leave the bedroom, the door opened and Hollie walked in. "Everyone will be here soon."

"Sarah and Matt too?"

A smile played at the corners of her mouth. "Mom, Lucy, and Sarah were able to do a reverse spell on him and he's back to his normal self. Or at least, Sarah thinks he is. Once they were finished, he went to sleep. Woke up on Sarah's sofa, told her that she and her family are insane, and then stormed out."

I shook my head.

"Guess he's going to deny the magick and keep fighting against it," I said. "I wonder why, though. Why is he so hell bent on refusing to acknowledge it?"

"And you?" Hollie asked, her eyes so hopeful-looking that I couldn't ignore it any longer.

"I accept it, Hollie."

"You do?" she asked as she crossed the room and stood before me.

With a single nod, I replied, "I do."

"What changed your mind?"

I swallowed the lump in my throat. "That vision. Then the locket appearing in my hand."

"You could have picked it up from the site and not realized it."

Lifting a brow, I asked, "Are you now saying I don't have some kind of gift?"

"No, not at all. I think you do."

"I'm not really sure what to do with all this," I said.

Hollie shrugged. "Nothing, if you want. It's up to you."

I leaned in and kissed her on the forehead. "You know I love you so very much."

She tilted her head and smiled up at me. "I do know that. And you know I love you more than the air I breathe."

"I do know that."

She took my hands. "Come on, let's go out back."

Figuring she wanted to show me the set up for the Fourth of July party we were throwing later that day, I followed.

We stepped outside, and I drew in a deep breath. It wasn't very hot for July, and the air felt crisp. I glanced up to see if a storm was about to move in.

We sat down on the outdoor sofa, and Hollie squeezed my hand. "What did you want to talk to me about?"

Giving her a confused look, I asked, "What do you mean?"

"Yesterday, my mom said you wanted to talk to me."

I laughed. "That's right. The mom intuition thing."

She winked.

"Hollie, do you really think that our baby is the reincarnation of someone in your family tree?"

"I don't know," she replied with a shrug. "Does it matter if she is?"

"No, but that vision was so damn real. I felt like I was in that room with her. And when she called me daddy—I don't know. I've been rattled ever since."

"Here's what I think. After Charlotte's home was discovered and you showed up, it created a connection to the past. So Charlotte used your magick to take you there."

I rubbed at the back of my neck. "But why?"

"Maybe she wanted you to see something or know something."

"About her?"

"Possibly. Or maybe it was about how she died."

I drew in my brows as I let that sink in.

"Did you notice anything in the vision?"

"No. I mean, of course I noticed her and the doll she was holding. I'm pretty sure it was the same exact one we found at the site."

"Lucas, have you ever thought about why you wanted to be an archeologist?"

Hollie's question caused me to take a moment to truly think about it. "I love history and discovering things that have been lost."

She smiled. "Have you opened the locket yet?"

With a shake of my head, I replied, "No."

"Maybe we should open it."

Reaching into my pocket, I pulled the locket out and stared down at it. "What do you think is inside?"

"I'm not sure, but there's only one way to find out."

I drew in a deep breath and closed my eyes. The image of little Charlotte clutching her doll popped into my mind.

KELLY ELLIOTT

That's when I realized she had been wearing the locket all along. I opened my eyes and looked at Hollie.

"She was wearing the locket in the vision."

"That's not surprising; it was her locket."

"Right," I said as I shook my head to clear my thoughts. Without stalling any longer, I opened the locket and stared at the painted portrait inside. It was in near-perfect condition.

"What is it?" Hollie asked.

Blinking at it, I slowly looked up. "It's...you."

"What?" Hollie reached for the locket and then paused. "Every time I touch this locket, she moves."

"Hollie, look at the painting. It is you."

She glanced down and drew in a breath. Her eyes lifted to meet mine.

"Was this Charlotte's mother?" I whispered.

"I don't know. How do we find out? Who do we talk to, where do we go?"

Someone cleared their throat and we both looked up to see Hollie's mother, Elaine, standing there.

"Mom, what are you doing here?"

She smiled, walked over to us, and sat down on the table in front of the sofa.

Looking from Hollie to me, she drew in a breath and then slowly exhaled. "Charlotte's mother Elizabeth had a best friend named Sara Windsor. They were inseparable. I'm not sure if Sara had the gift of magick—it was only ever recorded in one place and the writing wasn't very clear. She never married, and she was like a second mother to Charlotte after Elizbeth died in childbirth. According to Charlotte's brother, Matthew, Sara wasn't the least bit sad when Elizbeth passed away in childbirth. Matthew wrote in his journal that she'd started to take it upon herself to care for John, Charlotte, and Matthew more and more. Apparently, Matthew overheard

Sara telling his father she was with child. She wanted him to marry her and to claim the child as his own."

"Was he the father?"

"No. When Matthew asked his father about it, he told his son that he'd never touched Sara. He couldn't do that to Elizbeth. In his journal, Matthew wrote that Sara became so enraged she threatened the entire family. He believed that Sara set fire to the homestead. He could never prove it, but he made a vow to his little sister that he would find out who killed her and their father. Matthew stated that a man from London named William Merlin showed up in Salem not long after. He was wealthy and looking for a wife to care for his young daughter after his own wife had died on their voyage across the ocean. Sara must have convinced him to marry her."

Hollie's mouth dropped open. "Merlin?"

Elaine nodded. "Matthew wrote that Sara was hellbent on condemning women she didn't like, accusing them of being witches or whores. She had a rather nasty reputation in the community. According to Matthew's journal, William Merlin had an affair with another woman, and Sara claimed she was a witch after finding out about it. I'm assuming that hatred for all things witch-related was passed down from generation to generation. Matt is still carrying on that tradition, although it has lessened with each generation."

"Could Sara have placed a spell on all future generations?" I asked. "I mean, if she herself was a witch."

"Lucy thinks so. She believes that Sara, or someone else at her urging, put a spell on future generations of Merlins, making them despise anyone who practices witchcraft. Matt's father is the same way, though his dislike isn't as powerful as Matt's is. Lucy and Sarah seem to think that his love for his wife has softened him over the years."

"Love is more powerful than hate," Hollie stated.

I was suddenly transported to the past when a memory hit me out of nowhere. It was of Matt teasing and flirting with Sarah.

"Matt liked Sarah when we were younger," I said. "I remember his father telling him to stay away from her and her family."

Hollie gasped. "Because his father had a spell cast on him so he wouldn't like our family."

Mom nodded. "Even if a spell had been placed on Matt, his attraction for Sarah was too strong. The family moved away from Salem, but I don't believe Matt's father ever truly wanted to leave."

"It was the spell," Hollie whispered. "Attempting to separate the two of them."

"They were destined to be together—there's no doubt about it. When you girls cast that spell to make Lucas recognize his gifts, it also hit Matt. But not in the way we thought. We all just assumed he was a witch as well."

"But what about his wishes coming true?" I asked.

"At first, Lucy, Sarah, and I all thought it had something to do with four of you casting the spell instead of three. It was too powerful."

"Four?" I asked, looking at Hollie.

Smiling, she placed her hand on her stomach. "Charlotte."

I couldn't help but smile in return.

"But once Lucy figured out that Sarah still had feelings for Matt, we realized that her part of the spell was just that—a spell. Matt was under a spell. Everything he wished for came true. He wasn't making them come true, the spell was."

I laughed and shook my head. "That's insane."

"It makes sense," Hollie said. "When we cast the spell, I wished that Lucas would accept his gift, and Sarah was supposed to be doing the same thing. But if she thought about

Matt at any point, she probably wished for him to accept her or like her again. With his hair in the spell, it would have done just that."

Elaine laughed. "I'll say. Matt is back to his normal self, with the exception of one thing."

"What?" Hollie and I asked at the same time.

"He no longer has a distaste for witches. I think the truth spell meant for Lucas cancelled out the spell that had been placed on Matt's family years ago."

Hollie smiled. "Oh, that is wonderful news! And him and Sarah?"

With a smile of her own, Elaine replied, "Last I saw, they were tucked away in a corner talking— and from the way they looked at one another, they weren't arguing."

Hollie and I exchanged a look.

"This is wonderful!" Hollie said. "Everything worked out perfectly, just like I knew it would!"

Elaine and I both looked at her and then started to laugh.

Frowning, my beautiful wife got up, turned on her heels, and marched away.

"How long do you think it'll be before my wife finds her next victim, I mean subject, to cast one of her *helpful* spells on?"

With a laugh, Elaine said, "Call it a witch's intuition, but I don't think it'll be long."

I nodded. "Life with Hollie and Charlotte will never be dull."

When I turned to look at my mother-in-law, I saw that she was grinning at me. "A little bit of razzle dazzle to keep you on your toes."

I returned her smile. "And I wouldn't have it any other way."

Chapter Ten

Hollie

The Fourth of July party was a smashing success. With the spell on Matt's family finally broken, he couldn't take his eyes off of Sarah. Or leave her side. He was smitten, and I could tell Sarah was as well. I was so happy for my sister. It was about time she found someone who made her smile like that every day.

"How are you feeling?" Lucas asked, wrapping his arms around me and resting his chin on my shoulder.

"I'm doing good. I am getting tired, but I think I'll make it to the fireworks show."

He turned me around and looked down at me with nothing but love in his eyes. "Do you think anyone would notice if we snuck off so you could rest for a bit?"

Running my finger along his stubbled chin, I laughed. "I'm pretty sure they'll notice, but I'd still like to go sit down for a bit."

Lucas took my hand in his and led us into the house and to our bedroom.

"Sit down and I'll massage your feet."

Doing as he asked, I let out a moan of pleasure as Lucas worked his hands over my feet and up my calf muscles. It feel so good that I was positive if I dropped back onto the bed, I'd fall fast asleep.

A knock on the bedroom door caused me to let out a scream. Lucas chuckled and told whoever it was to come in.

Kristin popped her head in. "What are you doing?" she asked, looking at me with a confused expression.

"I needed to take a break; I was feeling tired."

Her eyes went to my stomach and then she looked up and met my gaze. With a nod, she said, "I imagine you are." She crinkled her nose. "Please tell me you didn't sneak off to have sex."

Lucas laughed. "We didn't."

"Did you come searching for us for a reason?" I asked.

"As a matter of fact, I did."

I stared at her for a few moments before I asked, "Well?"

"Who was responsible for bringing the fireworks?"

Closing my eyes, I counted to five before focusing back on my best friend. "That would be you and Shawn."

She had a blank expression on her face. "Right. I was simply making sure you knew that. That I brought them. Because I'm a reliable friend."

I nodded.

Kristin cleared her throat. "Okay. So, I'm going to go run a quick errand."

I gaped at her. "Kristin, please tell me you did not forget to bring them!"

With a wide grin, she replied, "I won't tell you that."

Turning to leave, she stopped and looked back at me. "And don't worry! I did buy some, I just left them at home!"

"That makes me feel better."

"Oh good! Then what I'm about to tell you next won't make you so mad."

My smile faded.

"I kinda told Matt and Sarah that Shawn and I could beat them at chicken."

"Chicken?" Lucas and I asked at the same time.

"You know, when you get in a pool and get on a guy's shoulder and wrestle."

"I know what chicken is, Kristin!" I exclaimed. "We don't have a pool."

Letting out a nervous bubble of laughter, she replied, "That is true, and apparently it's not a good idea to play it in a backyard full of people."

All I could do was stare at her, wondering what in the hell just happened.

"By the way, you no longer have that cute little Fourth of July cake. And funny thing, I apparently do not have the magickal powers to conjure up a new cake. Neither does Sarah."

My eyes went wide. "You ruined my cake!"

Taking a few steps away and holding up her hands, she said, "Truth be told, Hollie, you put on a great party, but your baking sucks, so it's really a win-win for all of us!"

Before I could reply, she started to walk away. Calling over her shoulder, she shouted, "I'll pick up a new cake, don't worry!"

Following her, I shouted back, "Nothing's open today!"

I leaned back into Lucas and stared up at the night sky, watching the fireworks show the city of Salem was putting on. With every loud boom of a firework, Charlotte gave a little startled jump.

"Do you think she's okay?" Lucas asked, his hand on my stomach.

"I think so. She isn't jumping as badly anymore."

Yawning, I dropped my head against his shoulder.

"Do you want to call it a night?" he asked.

"As much as I've loved today, I think I'm ready to head home."

Lucas slid out from behind me and stood. He helped me up, and I glanced over to see Matt and Sarah snuggled up under a nearby tree.

"Look at them," I said. "They're not even watching the fireworks; they're making out like two high school kids!"

Lucas followed my gaze and laughed. "Cut them some slack, Hollie. It's been a long time coming."

I watched Lucas gather up our blanket. Kristin and Shawn were lying down on a blanket next to ours, and both simply waved when we said we were leaving. Kristin told us to leave the blanket since they'd grab everything when they left.

"Should we tell the love birds we're going?" I asked.

"Nah," Lucas replied. "Let them have their fun."

My house wasn't far from the park that we'd decided to go to when Kristin had failed to return with any fireworks. Lucas took my hand in his and we fell into conversation as we started to walk home.

"Do you ever get scared?" he asked me.

"I get scared all the time, but are you talking about something specific?"

He chuckled. "The baby. The closer we get, the more scared I'm getting. What if she comes out talking?"

I let out a burst of laughter. "She's not going to."

"That vision or dream or whatever it was felt so real, Hollie. It really freaked me out."

"I know it did. There's a reason it happened, though, and maybe it all had to do with Matt showing up in town?"

"Maybe, but I don't think so."

We kept walking as the fireworks behind us sped up into the finale before slowly stopping. Soon, all I could hear were crickets.

"Hollie?"

"Yeah?" I asked, looking up at the stars in the sky while we walked.

"Look where we are."

Dropping my head, I stared at the dig site before me.

"Mr. Payton, what brings you by so late?" asked the police officer who was standing guard at the archaeological site.

"We were just out for a walk, and I wanted to make sure all was well," Lucas stated.

The officer nodded and unlocked the gate to the fence that had been put up around the entire site.

Lucas took my hand, and we started toward the house.

"Lucas, why are we here?" I asked.

"I'm not sure," he said as guided me closer to the rock foundation of the house. "Watch your step, Hollie."

My eyes widened as I stared at the site before me. It was Charlotte's house. The home where she'd lived and died.

Placing my hand over my stomach, I wondered what had brought us here. It wasn't a mere coincidence we'd ended up walking here instead of going straight home.

"Come on, let me show you where we found the doll," Lucas said before he went back to ask the officer if he could borrow his flashlight.

We walked over to where the team had clearly been focusing on digging. Lucas stopped and stared down at the ground.

"What is it?" I asked.

"Did she suffer?" he whispered. "Charlotte. When she was in this house and it was on fire. I pray she didn't suffer."

I glanced around, longing to bend down and touch one of the old stones. But I knew I couldn't since it was a sensitive area.

Then suddenly it felt like I was on a ride, dipping and spinning as my heart dropped to the ground.

Lucas and I were standing in an old house that wasn't very large. There was a fire going in the hearth and I could hear what sounded like a chair rocking back and forth. Dropping Lucas's hand, I turned and gasped. A little girl sat in rocking chair, holding a baby doll.

"Charlotte," I whispered.

She glanced up and smiled. "You came! I've been waiting!"

Lucas took hold of my hand again and whispered, "Do you see her too?"

Nodding, I led us both across the old wood plank floors. Stopping right in front of her, I bent down. The smell of smoke was overwhelming, but I couldn't see any flames.

"Do you smell smoke?" I whispered.

Lucas squeezed my hand. "Yes, but I only see the fire in the hearth."

"Is that our dolly?" I asked as I pointed to it.

Charlotte nodded her head. "Tis. My mama gave it to me. The bad woman hurt Papa, and she locked me in here. She told me I was going to go see my mama, but the smoke burns my eyes."

Lucas jumped up and looked around. "Holy shit."

I turned to see a woman starting a fire in the corner of the small house. A man was on the floor, clearly passed out.

"She's starting the fire, Lucas," I whispered.

Turning back at Charlotte, I said, "Give me your hand, darling girl, and we'll get you and your papa out of here."

With a look that said she was much wiser than her years, Charlotte shook her head. "I cannot. But I need you to take her."

She held out the doll. "Save it for me, please."

"What?" I asked. "No, Charlotte, you have to come with me and Lucas."

Charlotte held out the doll. "Please take it. I'm running out of time."

I went to reach for her hand, but mine own went right through her. Was I dreaming? Was Charlotte a ghost?

Trying for her hand once again, I started to sob.

"Lucas! Lucas, I can't get hold of her! We have to get her out of her! Lucas!"

He put his hand on my shoulder and calmly said, "Hollie, take the doll."

The steady way he spoke had me drawing in a breath and looking back at Charlotte.

Blue eyes met mine, and I froze. "Tis real, this one," she said. "Tis the one you must take care of for me."

With shaking hands, I reached for the doll. Charlotte put it in my arms and then smiled.

"I'll see you soon, Mama and Papa. I'm going to sleep now."

Squeezing my eyes shut, I frantically shook my head. When I opened my eyes again, I was standing in the same spot as before, staring down at where the house once stood.

I turned to Lucas. "What was that? Was I dreaming just now?"

He slowly shook his head then looked down at my hand. When I followed his gaze, I gasped.

"The doll."

Lucas screwed up his face in confusion. "How is this possible? That doll is in a locked containment box to preserve it."

Clutching the doll to my chest, I looked into his eyes. "I'm not giving it to you."

He drew back like I'd just slapped him.

"I'm not, Lucas. Charlotte gave this to me to keep for her. I'm keeping it."

Scrubbing a hand down his face, Lucas started to pace. "I don't understand what in the hell is going on, Hollie. What's happening? I could get on board with the spells, but traveling back in time? I felt the heat from the fire, for fuck's sake!"

"So could I, but when I tried to touch her, it was like she was air. Like she wasn't there."

Lucas sighed. "We know how she died. Sara did it. How could she kill a child?"

I wiped a tear from my eye. "I'm not sure, but we need to get home and you need to figure out if the other doll is still there."

He gave me a strange look. "Of course it is, Hollie. It's in a locked case at the building where we store all of the artifacts we find in Salem. It's safe."

Raising a single brow, I asked, "Is it?"

Chapter Eleven

Lucas

Staring down at the glass box, I studied the doll that had been discovered at the dig site. It was an exact duplicate of the doll that was currently under Hollie's protection at our home. The day after Hollie and I had gotten the doll, I'd brought it into the lab and had Tripp run several tests on it, including x-raying it—all of the same tests we'd done previously to the doll I was currently looking at.

"What do you make of it?" Matt asked.

Hollie and I had told Matt, Sarah, and Tripp about what had happened to us. Hollie hadn't wanted to tell Tripp for fear he'd think she'd taken the doll from the site. But Tripp had completely believed our story and was eager to find out if the two dolls were identical or not.

"I don't know. How are there two dolls?" I replied.

"That's your question?" Matt asked with a laugh. "You don't think the fact that you and your wife traveled back in time and got a doll that's a few hundred years old from a little girl who was already dead isn't the bigger question here?"

Sighing, I nodded. "Yeah, that part is crazy as well. I'm honestly wondering if I'm in a dream."

"How do you think I feel? I found out my great, great, four times or whatever grandmother put a goddamn hex on our family. She also killed a man and his daughter because she was angry he wouldn't marry her. And I'm in love with a witch. A real witch."

Turning to look at him, I found myself chuckling. "You've had a busy few days, there's no doubt about it."

He smiled. "Did you run tests on the doll?"

Turning away from the case, I leaned against the table. "We did. It's authentic, as far as we can tell, and exactly the same as the one in this case."

Matt looked around to make sure no one was listening. "Do you really think the doll Hollie has is from the 1700s? That you traveled back in time? What if Hollie conjured it up somehow? Put a spell on the both of you or something?"

I shook my head. "I think something led us there. Hollie needed to be with me at that site for us to go back together. Charlotte was meant to give Hollie the doll. The first time I saw her, she was holding the same doll. The house wasn't on fire, but she didn't try to give it to me then."

"I have to tell you, Lucas, this all sounds crazy to me. I'm still trying to wrap my head around it all, and now you're throwing all of this at me this morning?"

Pushing off the table, I walked out of the room and Matt followed. I entered the code to lock the door and then we proceeded to walk in silence to my office. When I stepped inside, I found Tripp waiting for me.

"Well?" I asked as I walked around my desk.

"The doll dates back to the same time period as the one we found at the site."

Matt looked between me and Tripp. "You told Tripp! You're going to lose your job, Lucas."

Tripp laughed. "Not because of me." Turning back to me, he added, "There was something that we found under the x-ray, though. It's so worn that we couldn't see it with the naked eye."

"What was it?" Matt and I asked at the same time.

"Someone carved something onto the doll." He handed me a photo and I stared down at it.

Elizbeth.

"That was her mother's name," I whispered as I looked up at Tripp. "According to the journal we have from Charlotte's brother, she got this doll from her mother."

"The doll from the dig site doesn't have this carving in it. I went back and had them do more x-rays just to make sure."

"So the doll that Hollie has is the one that belonged to Charlotte and her mother," I said. "Then what doll do we have?"

A knock on my door had the three of us turning to see Mary Flanagan, the manager of the storage area where all the artifacts are kept, standing there with a stern expression on her face.

"Mary, what's wrong?" I asked.

"You didn't log it out, Lucas. You know better than to take an artifact and not log it out."

Confused, I asked, "What are you talking about?"

"The doll from the Plymouth Street dig site."

Matt and I exchanged a look before I turned back to her. "I don't have the doll. I never even took it out of the case."

Her eyes went wide. "Okay, well, then do you want to explain to me why you were looking at it only moments ago and now it's gone?"

"What do you mean it's gone?" I asked, pushing past everyone and running out of my office to the storage area. I frantically typed in the security code and rushed into the large room. Then I made my way to the box and stared down at it.

"It's gone," Matt whispered. "How in the hell is it gone?"

Trip went to open the case. "It's still locked."

I faced Mary, my heart nearly pounding out of my chest. "Mary, can you pull up the security cameras? Do it for the last hour."

"Yes, follow me—I can access it from my computer."

Ten minutes later, the four of us were watching the footage.

"Matt should be walking up any second," I said.

Pointing to the computer monitor, Matt said, "There, here I come."

We watched as Matt and I spoke. I turned and leaned against the table, we spoke for a few more minutes, and then we both walked out of the room. A light from the box suddenly nearly lit up the entire room, and when it dimmed out, the doll was gone.

"What in the hell was that?" Matt whispered.

Mary covered her mouth with her hand and mumbled, "That's impossible. It's impossible."

Tripp looked at me with a stunned expression on his face.

"Where's the doll? Where did it go? What was that light? No one is going to believe this!" Mary said in a rushed voice.

"Play that back and record it, Mary," I said as I started to pace. How in the hell could something like that go missing? The security we had for that case was extensive.

"Could it be a trick of the light? Maybe someone used the light to distract the cameras, and they somehow got the doll?" Matt asked.

"No, look at the door—no one came in or out after you and Lucas left. Then I walked into the room right as the light vanishes," Mary stated.

On screen, we watched Mary walk into the room. "The motion sensory went off, which was why I went into the room at all," Mary stated. Her image looked around at a few things before turning to look at the doll.

"That's when I noticed it was gone! Right then!"

I kept pacing, trying to think of any other possible way the doll could have disappeared. Then I remembered something Charlotte had said to Hollie in the vision or dream or whatever it had been.

"Tis real, this one. Tis the one you must take care of for me."

"That wasn't the doll she wanted us to have," I murmured.

"Who?" Mary asked.

Looking up at the three of them, I smiled. "It was magick. There must have been a spell on that doll. It was the key that allowed Charlotte to contact me and Hollie."

"It was the portal," Matt stated. "It had to be. Sarah told me that's how you guys traveled back in time."

"Dude," Tripp said, a wide smile on his face. "That's some cool shit."

Mary glanced around at all of us. "What in the hell are the three of you talking about! We have a missing three-hundred-year-old doll and you're talking about magick and portals?" She leaned in and sniffed. "Have you been...you know... smoking the reefer? Dope? Mary Jane?"

When we all stared at her as she went on. "Hash, pot, grass, dope?"

"You said that one already," Tripp pointed out. "Are you sure you're not the one smoking the...reefer?"

Rolling her eyes, Mary crossed her hands over her chest and stared at me. "Are you trying to tell me that the doll just up and vanished on its own because it had a spell on it?"

I nodded.

"A magic spell?" Mary asked with a disbelieving laugh.

"Magick, yes," I replied.

She burst out laughing.

Matt attempted to hide his smile and failed while Tripp frowned. "Mary, how else do you explain what happened?"

She stopped laughing and thought for a moment. "I can't explain it. That doesn't mean I think it was cursed."

"Not cursed, Mary. Magick," I repeated.

Blinking rapidly, Mary asked, "Lucas Payton, are you being serious? Are you saying that someone didn't come up with some elaborate hoax to steal the doll? You truly believe it was...it was..."

Swallowing hard, she whispered, "A spell?"

I gave her a wink said, "Now, Mary, tell me you're not afraid of a little bit of hocus pocus."

She took a step back, looked at us each, turned to the monitor, and watched the doll disappear again.

"No one is going to believe this." She shook her head. "Magick."

Watching the video replay on a loop, I smiled. "Magick."

Chapter Twelve – Hollie

"Here you go!" I said as I dropped the last candy bar into the trick-or-treater's bag. "The last one!"

The little girl squealed in delight and ran to her waiting mother and father.

Shutting the door, I set the empty bowl down and wobbled into the living room. Lucas looked up and smiled as he patted the seat next to him.

"Come here and let me massage your feet."

"She's late, Lucas."

"I know, baby, but you're going in tomorrow to be induced. You could have done it yesterday."

"And have her be born on Halloween? No."

"What's wrong with Halloween?"

Sighing, I dropped my head back and moaned when he worked his fingers into my aching arches.

"Nothing is wrong with Halloween. I just don't want my daughter born on it. She'll want Halloween themed parties half her life."

Lucas laughed. "That's a bad thing?"

I shrugged and met his gaze. "No. I'm sorry, I'm so tired and I feel like I've been pregnant forever!"

Charlotte gave a hard kick and I jumped. "She has your temperament."

Placing his hand on my swollen belly, Lucas said, "Don't be so hard on your mom, Charlotte. She's been working hard at feeding and keeping you warm."

I smiled when I saw a little foot push against my stomach.

"I'll never get used to that," Lucas said with a chuckle.

He massaged my feet for a few more minutes before I exhaled and said, "I'm craving some Swedish Fish."

Lucas gagged. "How can you eat that crap?"

"I can't help it if you don't have good taste."

When I stood, I heard Lucas draw in a loud breath of air. Turning to look at him, I saw a wet spot on the sofa.

"Oh my gosh, did I pee on the sofa?"

Lucas flew up, stared down at the sofa, and screamed, "Holy shit!"

With a roll of my eyes, I said, "It's not that big of a deal. I can use the small carpet cleaner or have Mom or Sarah clean it."

"Oh my God!" Lucas said, turning to look at me. His eyes went to my stomach, and he pointed. "It's...it's...it's..."

"Pee. Get used to it now," I said as I turned on my heels and walked toward the kitchen and my snack stash. "I heard that sometimes when you change the baby, they pee right then and there. Your mom said one time you peed so far it hit the ceiling fan and went everywhere."

"Hollie!" Lucas shouted, causing me to turn and look at him.

"What?"

"Your water broke!"

I looked down then back up. With a shake of my head, I said, "No."

He nodded.

"No," I repeated, whipping my head back and forth until it felt like it would snap off. "I cannot go into labor on Halloween!"

Lucas flew past me, nearly breaking his neck in the process. "The bag!"

"It's already in the car. Remember? I'm being induced tomorrow. This is all just a strange peeing incident. Let's go take a shower and..."

My voice trailed off as I saw Lucas come running back with his bag over his neck, a bag of Doritos in one hand, and his phone in the other.

"We need to call your mom!"

The doorbell rang then flew open as Sarah, my mother, and Lucy walked in.

"Elaine!" Lucas shouted. "Your daughter is about to have a baby!"

Talking control of my clearly psychotic husband, my mother took the bag off of his neck then pried the chips out of his hands.

"Sarah, go take this out to the car, will you sweetheart?" she said.

Doing as my mother asked, Sarah looked at me and raised a single brow. I shrugged.

"So your wife goes into labor and you thought she needed a bag of Doritos?" Sarah asked.

Lucas shot a look at my sister. "She loves them, okay!"

Holding up her hands, Sarah slowly backed out of the door.

"What are the three of you doing here?" I asked.

"We all sensed the baby was coming," Lucy stated.

"Oh no." I waved my hands across my front. "Not today. She's going to be born tomorrow, or November secohhhhh!"

"What's wrong?" Lucas asked, rushing to my side.

"I think I'm...having a...contraction—ohhhh...yep. Pain. Oh, that's painful."

Lucas went to pick me up then stopped. "I might trip. Can you walk, baby?"

I nodded. "Yes. But no, this isn't how it's supposed to be."

My mother laughed. "Not even you can control that, sweetheart. Come on. Let's get you to the hospital."

Once at the hospital, Lucas passed out, Sarah declared to the entire room that she was never having sex again, Lucy fell asleep on the sofa in the room, and my mother kept wiping a wet rag over my forehead.

"The contractions are getting closer. Goodness, you're moving along pretty quickly," Dr. Lenard stated after she did an exam. "I think you're ready to push."

Mom kissed me on the forehead and whispered, "Lucas is awake now. I'll let him take over."

Nodding, I gritted my teeth. The doctor had said there was no time for an epidural, so every time I had a contraction, my mother and Lucas would grimace when I squeezed their hands.

Lucas appeared and smiled down at me.

"You fainted," I panted out as the doctor said, "Give me a good push, Hollie."

He reached for my hand and clasped it tightly. "You didn't see what I saw. I'm not sure I'm ever going to be able to look at you down there again!"

The nurse next to Lucas cleared her throat and gave a quick little shake of her head as she whispered, "Other people in the room."

Lucas blushed then looked down at my hand. "Babe, can you maybe not squeeze it so hard? That hurts."

"Another push," the doctor said as gripped my husband's hand harder and leaned forward to push.

I wasn't sure who was crying out louder, me or Lucas. Then the sounds of our baby's cries filled the air, and I dropped back against the pillows, exhausted.

Lucas cut the cord, the nurses cleaned off the baby, and before I knew it, she was on my chest looking up at me with the biggest blue eyes I'd ever seen.

"Welcome to the world, Charlotte Elizbeth Payton."

I felt tears streaming down my face as Lucas leaned over and kissed me on the temple. I turned my head to see that he was crying as well. He kissed me softly on the lips then looked down at our daughter.

"She's the most beautiful little girl I've ever laid eyes on."

Charlotte stared into her father's eyes then looked back up at me. I swore she was looking into my soul.

"Charlotte, are you able to say dada?" Lucas asked as all eyes went to him.

I closed my eyes and shook my head.

"Um, that won't be for a few more months, Lucas," Dr. Lenard said, clearly trying not to smile.

Lucas and I stared down at our little girl. Suddenly, she smiled. If we hadn't been looking right at her, we would have missed it.

"She smiled!" Lucas and I both cried out.

"That's just gas, sweetheart," one of the nurses stated.

Looking back down at my daughter, I giggled and whispered, "Working your magick already, are you?"

Lucas huffed. "Oh sure, she'll do *that* before she says dada!"

Epilogue

Hollie
Six Years Later

"You cheated, Charlotte!"

"Girls don't cheat!" my daughter spat back at her cousin Ryan. He was one year younger than she was, but the two of them were inseparable. They were playing some game they'd made up while Matt and Lucas stood by and watched.

We hadn't seen any signs that either Charlotte or Ryan had the gift, but Charlotte often spoke of memories that were clearly not from this century.

After Charlotte tired of Ryan and accused him of being a boy, she made her way over to me. She climbed up in the chair next to me and smiled.

"Are you having fun?" I asked.

She nodded.

"Are you excited for the fireworks?"

Another nod. She glanced around and asked, "Where's my dolly?"

"Right here," I stated as I reached to my other side and produced the doll that was wrapped up in a blanket.

Charlotte smiled and ran her finger lightly over its cheek. "Mama?"

My heart jumped at the name Charlotte would sometimes call me. Most of the time, I was mommy and Lucas was daddy, but every once in a while she would call us mama and papa.

"Yes?"

"When I was waiting to come to you and Daddy, I used to talk to my first mama."

I brushed a stray blonde curl from her face. "Did you? What did you talk about?"

She smiled. "Mama liked you. I did too."

My heart felt as if it might burst in my chest. "I'm so glad. I'd be lost without you, Charlotte. I'm so happy you came to me."

Glancing up, her little smile faded. "It was so hot, and I was so afraid dolly would be hurt. But you and Daddy came and saved her from the fire."

I fought to hold back my tears. "Do you remember that?"

She nodded. "I don't want to remember it."

Lucas came over and bent down in front of Charlotte. The connection the two of them shared sometimes made me jealous. I'd see them playing together, and they'd look as if they were off in another time. But the feeling of jealousy always disappeared quickly. Charlotte and I were both so lucky to have someone like Lucas in our lives. He was the best father and husband anyone could ask for, and we both loved him dearly.

"Do you want to go swimming?" Lucas asked.

Charlotte lit up. "Yes! Yes, Daddy, yes!" Turning to me, she asked, "Will you and Michael come swimming too?"

"Michael?" I asked in confusion. Charlotte nodded and pointed to my flat stomach. "Yes, Michael. He wants to go swimming too!"

My eyes snapped up. Lucas raised a single brow and shrugged.

"Charlotte, who is Michael?" I asked as she stood up and carefully wrapped her dolly in her blanket and deposited her safely onto her chair.

Glancing up at me, she said, "My baby brother!"

Charlotte took Lucas's hand and started to pull him toward the pool.

"Come on, Mommy and Daddy! Let's swim!"

I pressed both hands went to my stomach as I stood up and looked at Lucas.

"Are you?" he softly asked, letting Charlotte pull him toward the pool we had put in two years ago at the house we'd bought just before Charlotte was born.

"I don't know! I'm a few weeks late, but I haven't taken a test yet."

Charlotte dropped Lucas's hand and started to jump in excitement. "Mommy, Daddy! Come on! Jonathon is ready to go swimming too!"

My mouth fell open, and Lucas took a few steps back. When we looked at one another, we both laughed.

"Twins?" he asked.

"There's no way!"

At that moment, Kristin came walking into the backyard with Shawn behind her and their two-year-old daughter Kate on his shoulders. She stopped in front of me, kissed me on the cheek, then took a step back. Looking from me to Lucas, she let out a scream. That caused Kate to start screaming and then Charlotte joined in.

"Oh my God! Oh my God!"

I shot a disbelieving look at Lucas before turning back to Kristin.

"Okay, please don't say anything!" I begged. After all, I hadn't even taken a pregnancy test.

"Don't say anything!" Kristin yelled as she gaped at me. "I have to, Hollie!"

Before I could say another word she cried out, "You cut your hair and dyed it! What *were* you thinking!"

Lucas and I both looked at each other and laughed.

"This family is crazy," he said as he pulled me to him and kissed me.

Smiling, I replied, "Just a bit."

And they all lived happily ever after!

Other Books by Kelly Elliott

Other Books by Kelly Elliott
Holidaze in Salem
A Bit of Hocus Pocus
A Bit of Holly Jolly
A Bit of Wee Luck
A Bit of Razzle Dazzle

Love in Montana
Fearless Enough
Cherished Enough
Brave Enough – August 29, 2023
Daring Enough – November 21, 2023
Loved Enough – February 6, 2024
Forever Enough – April 30, 2024
Enchanted Enough – July 23, 2024
Perfect Enough – October 15, 2024
Devoted Enough – January 7, 2025

The Seaside Chronicles
Returning Home*
Part of Me*
Lost to You
Someone to Love - January 3, 2023
*Available on audiobook at time of print

Stand Alones

The Journey Home*
Who We Were*
The Playbook*
Made for You*
*Available on audiobook

Boggy Creek Valley Series

The Butterfly Effect*
Playing with Words*
She's the One*
Surrender to Me*
Hearts in Motion*
Looking for You*
Surprise Novella TBD
*Available on audiobook

Meet Me in Montana Series

Never Enough*
Always Enough*
Good Enough*
Strong Enough*
*Available on audiobook

Southern Bride Series

Love at First Sight*
Delicate Promises*
Divided Interests*
Lucky in Love*
Feels Like Home *
Take Me Away*
Fool for You*
Fated Hearts*
*Available on audiobook

Cowboys and Angels Series

*Lost Love**
*Love Profound**
*Tempting Love**
*Love Again**
*Blind Love**
*This Love**
*Reckless Love**
*Available on audiobook

Boston Love Series

Searching for Harmony
Fighting for Love
*Series available on audiobook

Austin Singles Series

Seduce Me
Entice Me
Adore Me
*Series available on audiobook

Wanted Series

*Wanted**
*Saved**
*Faithful**
Believe
*Cherished**
*A Forever Love**
The Wanted Short Stories
All They Wanted
*Available on audiobook

Love Wanted in Texas Series

Spin-off series to the WANTED Series

Without You

Saving You

Holding You

Finding You

Chasing You

Loving You

Entire series available on audiobook

*Please note *Loving You* combines the last book of the Broken and Love Wanted in Texas series.

Broken Series

*Broken**

*Broken Dreams**

*Broken Promises**

Broken Love

*Available on audiobook

The Journey of Love Series

Unconditional Love

Undeniable Love

Unforgettable Love

*Entire series available on audiobook

With Me Series

Stay With Me

Only With Me

*Series available on audiobook

Speed Series

Ignite

Adrenaline

*Series available on audiobook or coming to audiobook soon

COLLABORATIONS

Predestined Hearts (co-written with Kristin Mayer)*

Play Me (co-written with Kristin Mayer)*

*Dangerous Temptations (*co-written with Kristin Mayer*

*Available on audiobook